Me Tarzan You Dead

Peg Kay

The Washington Academy of Sciences was incorporated in 1898 as an affiliation of eight Washington D.C. area scientific societies. The founders included Alexander Graham Bell and Samuel Langley, Secretary of the Smithsonian Institution. Then as now, the purpose of the new Academy is to encourage the advancement of science and "to conduct, endow, or assist investigation in any department of science."

Over the past decade the publishing industry has undergone dramatic changes. The old, proud publishing houses have, for the most part, become virtually indistinguishable from other commercial establishments, delegating their traditional editorial functions to agents whose primary purpose is to meet the demands of the market. Increasingly, authors are eschewing the agent-to-publisher-to-mass market route and are turning to on-demand, self- publishing. That is, the book is written, formatted, uploaded to an on-demand publisher such as Amazon, and offered to the public. Often, editorial niceties and fact-checking have no place in the process.

This has led to a number of problems, the worst of which is – from the Academy's point of view –the great increase in "junk science" being published.

The Academy therefore offers those Academy members who have written a science-heavy book and intend to self-publish with an on-demand publisher, the opportunity to submit the book to our editors for review *of the science therein.* The manuscript receives the same rigorous scientific review that we accord articles published in our Journal. If the reviewer(s) determine(s) that the science is accurate, the author may then continue with the self-publishing process and the book will be issued under the imprint of the Washington Academy of Sciences. In cases where the Academy editors determine that the book is scientifically accurate but requires editing, they may return the manuscript to the author and request that it be satisfactorily edited.

The Academy stands behind the science in every book issued under its imprint. Other material therein is the responsibility of the author.

ISBN-13: 978-0615635842 LCCN: 2012907533

To Bob and Leslie Ayres:

without whom this novel would have been an inaccurate mess.

And

To Kathryn Johnson of Write by You:

Without whom this novel would have been a plotless mess.

And

To Sethanne Howard:

Without whom this novel would have been a syntactical mess.

I love you guys.

PREVIEW

THE OBJECT CODE

a computer program file -- usually a fragment --
that must be linked to the rest of the program to be understood

March 9, 1990

I was shivering up there on the roof, wedged between Don and Lee Roy in the space allotted to the non-performing members of the Laboratory for Industrial Technology staff. We were all a little nervous, all very chilly. That ass Delamain kept mumbling about how nice and brisk it was.

Our group was situated on the near left of the stairs coming up. The Members of the Subcommittee stood toward the far left, joined by the Subcommittee staff and the Department of Trade and Industry's Congressional liaison. The NASA brass and the DoTI dignitaries were at the far right. I glanced over at the Subcommittee. Congressman Jaeklin seemed impervious to the chill. Good. I sneaked a peak at the Department's delegation. The Secretary looked frozen and murderous. Not good.

In the no-man's land between the Congress and the Executive, Hump was peering over his belly at the stack of 3x5 crib cards we had prepared for him.

Don nudged me. "If the wind blows those cards out of his hands, we're dead."

Lee Roy leaned over. "Whad'd you say, Clyde?"

Me. “Shhhh.”

Hump was standing within a cut-away mockup of a space vehicle. DoTI's graphics department had done a superb job. The controls looked realistic, the 'hull' was heavy enough to withstand the occasional windy blasts, and the scale was big enough to comfortably hold Hump. I had the feeling that a real spacecraft cabin would have fit him like a sausage casing. As it was, he looked impressive -- framed nicely by the open door, the Washington Monument at a distance behind him.

At the near left of the roof, Alex was checking the cables to his micro. One last check. One last prayer. At the other end of the cables, in the center of the roof, were the robot arms; next to them was a table laden with various objects; at the far center left, a stool.

Hump cleared his throat loudly and began his speech. "I would like to thank you all for coming here when I know there are warmer, more comfortable places you would like to be. But we thought that you would -- well, never mind that". He turned to the next card.

Steve winced.

"Robot arms are essential to the performance of many tasks, uh, many tasks performed by our astronauts, who, uh, perform many tasks at a distance and require robot arms. So far, these arms have been single arms, each programmed to, uh, perform individual tasks. Devising a way to get two or more arms to work together has been a very stubborn problem -- a problem that NASA had been unable to solve -- at least until they came to my lab."

I looked over at the gaggle of Executive dignitaries. Now the NASA Administrator looked murderous.

Hump grinned. "When the two-armed robots go up in a spacecraft, they will be driven by much more sophisticated software than what we have here. And there won't be all these cables around for the astronauts to trip over. But the hard work has been done, and the rest is up to NASA. Turn it on, Alex." Hump put the unread cards in his jacket pocket and folded his arms across his paunch.

Alex typed the robot's name, 'Tarzan', onto the keyboard. The micro whirred, the cables transmitted the commands and the robot arms swung toward the table. One arm picked up a glass jar. The other arm moved in and deftly untwisted the cap. The arms set the jar and cap gently down on the table. Congressman Jaeklin applauded.

Unnoticed by the multitude, Alex made an 'aw, it was nuthin' gesture. He really was cute.

Now the arms swung toward their next task - the stool. Abruptly, they paused, changed direction, and accelerated toward the figure standing at the edge of the roof.

I closed my eyes. Opened them again. *Oh, my God, no! Stop!*

CHAPTER 1

December 20, 1989

Driving to work each day with a dead man has its advantages. For instance, as I weave through the tangle of Volvos attempting to kidnap my fenders...

"Whoa, Nellie! You maniac, owning a bleeping Volvo isn't a permit to scrape off my hubcaps!"

...he doesn't laugh at me. Doesn't patronize me even a little bit.

When I bitch about my job, which is often...

Do you want to hear some true lunacy? There's a Reduction in Force going on. A couple of top managers from agencies spend two mornings a week sitting on a RIF panel trying to protect their employees from bumps. And those guys are making nearly $100,000. Every time the budget gets cut, we have to make people go away. I bet you think we can get rid of deadwood. Think again. Unlike the real world, when people get fired they don't just leave. They have bumping rights, which means that they can shove other people out of their jobs, who shove other people out of their jobs, and so on. But they don't take a lower salary. No, no, no. For three years they keep the salary they got before they were RIFfed.

...he doesn't tell me to stop whining and get on with it.

There are also some disadvantages to driving to work each day with a dead man. For instance, he doesn't nuzzle my ear when we're stuck in traffic. He doesn't put his hand in untoward places at stop lights. And when I pull into a space in the parking lot down the block from the Laboratory for Industrial Technology - LIT - I don't get the snuggle-in-anticipation of more uxorious snuggles in the evening and into the night.

Dear God, Harry, how I wish you were still alive!

And on this bleak day in December, as on every other day, I sat in the car for a few minutes willing away the tears.

I took the elevator to the fifth floor, walked into my office and hung my coat on the back of the door. It isn't much of an office. Wood veneer desk. Lopsided bookcase. Chair that would have been a back-breaker if I hadn't brought one from home. The back-breaker is now reserved for whomever might drop into the office. There are windows looking out on a parking lot. Not my parking lot, alas. One reserved for the upper echelons.

I checked my in-box. On top was a fat package, attached to a note from my boss, Don Cromarty.

"You're on the Hit List. Write your defense for the panel meeting tomorrow a.m."

I peeked into the package and noted that Ivan Boobie, from DoTI's Statistics/Technical Analysis Bureau (STAB), was aimed squarely at my job. I laid the package in the center of my desk and headed for the staff meeting in Hump's conference room.

Lenore, Hump's secretary, was standing in front of the conference room door, a stack of files in her arms. "They're having a staff meeting in there."

"I know. You sent me a note."

Lenore sniffed. She was the only person I'd ever met who actually sniffed. "Well, the girl who had your job before you never came to the staff meetings."

"Well, the woman who has the job now does. If you'll excuse me, I'll join the stag party."

Lenore stepped out of the way. This time it was something between a snort and a sniff. I tried doing it as I walked into the conference room.

Don was in the room by himself. "Do you need a Kleenex?"

"No, I was just practicing."

Don looked puzzled then lit up. "Oh, Lenore. I can't do it either." We snorfed unsuccessfully at one another for a bit.

"D'ja get my note?"

I nodded. "And all that went with it. Donald, that is ridiculous. No one believes that Boobie can do my job. They tried him in a management job three years ago, and he screwed it up so badly he, his boss, his boss's boss, and for all I know the President, nearly went to jail. The only thing that saved them was his manifest incompetence. No one believed he had the brains to do it on purpose."

Don shrugged. "We can't defend by attacking his competence. They got him out of the job by giving him a silver medal and a 'promotion'."

"A silver? That carries at least $25,000 with it! Couldn't they have given him a bronze, for chrissake?"

"He already had a bronze for screwing up the job before that. Look, you know that when it comes to bumps it doesn't matter if the guy can't do the job; OPM only looks at whether he ever had it. So stop bitching and write the defense."

He winked at me. "Angie, over in DoTI's personnel office, gave me a copy of Boobie's file. That should help. Don't tell anyone you've got it."

"Got what?" Lee Roy slouched into the room and lowered his butt onto the chair at the right of the head of the table.

"An embarrassing social disease. I really don't want to discuss it, Lee Roy, it's too shaming."

"Awright. Awright. Hey, I got a good one about the nigger and the JAP. This nigger, see...."

John Delamain bustled in. "I've already heard it. Is Hump here yet?"

"No. He was pulling into the lot as I was walking out of it. He should be here any minute."

Stevie Chandler was right behind Delamain. He put his briefcase beside his chair. "Don, are you still looking for a car? I can get you a real deal."

"Is it hot?" Lee Roy asked.

"Don't ask," Steve said.

"Yeah, I'm still looking. But let's talk about it later. I hear Hump."

Humphrey Stafford clumped into the room, seated himself at the table's head. "Sorry I'm late. The schnauzer got away from me this morning, and I spent half an hour playing hide-and-seek with her. At least she was playing. Mauve couldn't help because she would have been late for her EST session."

Don rolled his eyes skyward.

Hump got up, walked over to the coffee pot and poured himself a cup. "Well, I guess we're all here. Let's get started."

The meeting room was a small cubicle lacking either grace or windows. A gray Formica-topped table and some mismatched, armless chairs defined the ambience. The people in the room comprised the top management staff of the Laboratory for Industrial Technology, a year-old agency within the year-old Department of Trade and Industry -- or DoTI. Hump Stafford was LIT's director. In his fifties, he was an overweight (almost grossly so) behemoth who had arrived at LIT from one of the Defense Department labs in Silicon Valley. There had been vague rumors about why he left the Defense job, but none of us had been able to pin them down as yet.

On the whole, we were pretty satisfied with Hump. His work habits were desultory, to put it mildly, but by and large he let us get on with our business without undue interference. There are worse things than a disinterested Director.

Hump was married to Mauve, the Compleat Airhead. She was about ten years, and pretended to be twenty years, younger than Hump. She was his second wife, and he was besotted. The rumor mill had it that Hump used to be a philanderer first class. If so, he must have been thinner. Or else I don't understand anatomy.

Don, the Director of Operations, sat next to Hump. Don wasn't the smartest guy in the world, the most even-tempered, thoughtful, or competent. But in the fifteen years of my working life, he was the best boss I'd had. He gave me assignments and he let me alone. If I did something dumb, he hollered at me but he did it in private. If I needed something, he made sure I got it. He was absolutely loyal to his staff and he expected absolute loyalty from them. From what I learned of his previous jobs, he had sometimes been disappointed in the latter regard. He was also a softball player. Right field. Don had a wife and two kids, all of whom he adored.

Steve Chandler, LIT's Executive Officer, officially reported to Don, though unofficially, he reported to me. Steve was a wonderful little guy, who always had a deal going. Need a car? His uncle was in the business. Relatives coming to town? His cousin owned a restaurant. Got some loose change? He knew this investment banker.

He was also in love. Always and often. And he invariably picked a short, dark, gorgeous barracuda who took him for lots of money before breaking it off. I'm not sure where he got the money they took him for but, as I said, he always had a deal going.

A rarity in a technical outfit such as LIT, Chandler was a fashion plate. This season's skinny trousers caused him some grief when he took to using a pocket-book for things that would normally go into trouser pockets. The techies heckled him until he shifted to a briefcase and began looking like an executive wannabe. Steve was only a quasi-member of the senior staff. He sat in on meetings about budget or administrivia, but when technical or program matters were discussed, he was banished back to his books.

Lee Roy Dubble was a red neck and a shit. An old timer, he transferred from someplace in the Department of Energy when LIT was created. He was classified as a computer specialist, a classification that signifies that he was supposed to know something about computers but didn't have the formal training required for the classification 'computer scientist'. He had convinced himself that LIT couldn't run without him and that he was Hump's heir apparent. Hump put him on the Director's Staff presumably because Lee Roy had an inexhaustible store of tasteless jokes and Hump liked tasteless jokes. We hadn't been able to figure out what else Lee Roy did.

John Delamain was another shit, but an urbane one. He held one of the four Senior Executive Service slots allotted to LIT. (Hump and Don hold two of the others. Francis Monk,

Chief Scientist, holds the fourth.)

Delamain was Technical Director and was supposed to ensure quality control. Like a lot of Federal bureaucrats, he didn't see the difference between saying something and doing something. For instance, when he announced his quarterly plans, they were well thought out, time-lined to a fare-thee-well, realistic, and useful. At the beginning of the next quarter, he announced a new set of quarterly plans, equally well thought out. And what was the result of the previous plans? Nothing. What were his troops doing all quarter? Working on the next set of plans, of course. Unlike Don, Delamain scapegoated . In the twenty years that John had been in the Federal Government, nothing had ever been his fault. No wonder he was promoted to the SES.

I, Beatrice Goode, am the remaining member of the senior staff. I've been a widow for three years, since our car got totaled in a collision with a drunk driver. Harry was killed. I had a miscarriage. Someday I suppose, I'll recover. Right now, my life ends each day after work. Don't ask about the weekends.

I'm classified as a senior economist. My job has nothing to do with economics, which is wonderful because I know nothing about economics. I also know nothing about industrial technology or trade. My functions at LIT include writing speeches, translating the engineers' reports into English, ensuring that LIT's organization is consistent with its mission, acting as designated meeting-goer, formulating budget strategies, showing visiting firemen around, and generally acting as Don's deputy. A doctorate in Management Science provides the background for the stuff I do. I bitch a lot but the job is fun.

Hump carried his coffee back to the table, slopping liquid as he went. "We might as well start with committee assignments." He riffled through some notes. "I got a note from the Secretary's office. They're putting up an inter-agency committee on export control. Defense is on it. State. The Trade Rep. DoTI is the lead agency; the Deputy Secretary is chairing, whatshisname, Gray. We're supposed to supply the technical rep. I'll take it."

"Aren't you too busy? I can do it." Delamain never missed a chance to rub shoulders with a Deputy Secretary.

"I'll take it," Hump repeated. "There's also a new interagency committee on Technology and Employment. Labor is lead. How about you, Bea?"

I looked over at John. He was studying his fingernails; probably no one important on that one. "O.K. Do we know when the first meeting is?"

"They'll let you know. Tell Lenore. Does anyone have anything else?"

Steve spoke. "The United Fund drive. We need someone to take charge. Can Ben do it, Bea?"

"He'd love it. He can gossip the whole day through as he makes his rounds. Remind me to tell him."

"We ought to talk about staff development," Steve said. "We gotta get some better courses."

"Isn't the Ada course any good? I took it and I learned a lot." Don looked aggrieved.

"That's not the point," Steve said. "You know how to program in other languages. This is the first course like that I've taken, and Ada ain't no computer language to start with. Ben and Lee Roy and I are sitting in there playing catch-up."

"You're playing catch-up, Clyde," Lee Roy said. "I'm just sittin' there jerkin' off and paddin' my credentials."

"Well, at least you were playing something. The problem is, I don't know how to do anything else on the computer. I'm the Executive Officer, and I don't know how to run a spreadsheet. Ada yes. Spreadsheet no. When the hell am I ever going to use Ada?"

"Look, Steve," Don sounded exasperated, "this is the end of a calendar year. You haven't taken anything else this year and you have to take a course. Ada is the course being given. When Lotus is given, you'll learn to use a spreadsheet. Meanwhile, learn what they give you, o.k.?"

Steve shrugged. "How was the course you just took at Santa Barbara?"

Don grinned. "I could stand to live out there. Actually, the course was pretty good. I know a lot more about robotics than I did before I took it. It might even come in handy with that NASA project."

"Let's get back to the agenda," Hump said. "Bea, are the performance reviews done?"

"I've done everyone except Ben. I've scheduled him this afternoon."

"Why do you keep that clown around?" Hump asked.

"Because he's good at his job, he works hard, and he'll take on any assignment he's asked to do."

"And he's a pain in the ass."

"That too."

"Alright. Let's get to the important stuff. The OMB budget mark came back."

We all straightened up. Even Lee Roy.

"It's lousy. Those bastards are cutting us by three million."

"Hump, we've only got six million. That leaves just about enough to close the doors. We can't take that budget."

"Well," said Hump, "we've got it."

"Jesus," Don said, "we better stop farting around here and do something. Bea, can you get to Congress?"

"I don't think so. All my contacts are on the old Science Committee. I don't think any of those guys came over to the new Trade and Industry subcommittee. I'll check, but don't hope high."

"We don't have any choice," Don said. "If you don't know 'em, meet 'em. No one else here has any Congressional contacts. It's important; the fact that we're gonna lose our jobs is the least of it. Without this Agency, we can kiss our chances for international high-tech trade dominance good bye."

"Do you really believe that, Clyde?" Lee Roy looked amused.

"Damn right." Don was not amused.

"I'll give it a shot," I said. "Who do I report to?"

"To Don," Hump said. "I don't want to know what you're doing on the Hill. If you get caught you'll get your wrists slapped. If I get caught, I'm canned."

"I'll stir up some industry support," Don said. "Do you want to know about that, Hump?"

"No."

"Steve, you're in charge of snooping. Find out what's going on at the Department. Will they support our protest? See if you can find out why the hell OMB did this?" Turning to Hump. "Do you want to know what Steve finds out?"

"Yeah."

"What about me?" asked Delamain. "What should I do?"

Don and I glanced at each other; looked away quickly.

"Well," said Hump, "you and Lee Roy really shouldn't do anything active. Someone around here has to maintain a semblance of normalcy. You guys do that. Incidentally, we have a new OMB analyst. He'll be here in January for a briefing -- just before the protests are heard. We'll talk about it when I get back. I'm going to Phoenix for a TIP meeting, and then Mauve and I are going to take a vacation. I'll be back January 4."

"What's TIP?"

Hump chuckled. "Trade and Industry Press. They have one great meeting a year, right before the holidays. Good food. Good booze. Classy resorts. They don't charge the people who take the publication service. Only costs us for travel. The seminars aren't usually so hot, but you can't have everything. I guess if the seminars were any good, we'd be tempted to get out of the pool and go to one or two. This way, no guilt feelings."

"Is that why we take that lousy publication service?"

"Shh," said Hump. "O.K., the last thing I want to talk about is the interagency fund transfer from NASA. Has that come through?"

"Yeah," said Don. "The money is here. Alex Carfil is running the project."

"Have Carfil brief us when I get back." Hump got up. "I think we're done."

As we made our way out of the little conference room I heard Lee Roy saying to Hump, "There was this nigger, see, and this JAP...."

"Jesus," Don remarked, "one of these days I'm gonna butcher Delamain. You ever notice how he wiggles out of every briefing when there's someone in the room who knows something? The bastard's a menace to God, Country, and Me."

"Cool it. Hump bothers me more. He ought to cancel that TIP meeting and prepare for the OMB briefing."

"Not if he wants to stay married to Mauve."

That comprises almost all of the cast of characters. Who would have thought that within a few months a member of that motley crew would turn out to be a killer.

CHAPTER 2

December 20, 1989 (cont.)

I walked into my office, stuck my tongue out at Boobie's file, and immediately walked back out to the office Ben shared with a phantom techie who spent all of his time on travel. The office was divided precisely in half by a bile-colored, shoulder-high partition. A connecting door led to Steve's office. Ben sat behind his desk, scowling at a disheveled mountain of papers. He was wearing an emerald green polyester suit, a blue and white checked shirt, and a tie emblazoned with Mickey Mouse. No tie tack.

"You'll never guess what Ginny Jean did to my report this time."

"Never in a million years."

Ben Goldfarb was a trade specialist. He probably knew more about the ins and outs of high-tech international trade than anyone else in the world, and the only thing preventing him from transferring his knowledge to the printed page was, according to Ben, an incredibly long line of incompetent secretaries.

"I told her to line up these columns. I even wrote the instructions down." He thrust a page full of incomprehensible scrawls at me. "See, I wrote it down for that idiot. But she still typed the thing straight across the page. How am I ever going to get this done?"

I successfully kept a straight face. "What are you working on now, Ben?"

Ben's eyes gleamed as he produced a neatly ruled page. "Well, what I'm doing is creating a method for rating the support staff so when you do their performance reviews you can base them on objective criteria."

I sank into the visitor's chair. Oh, Ben...

"It works like this, see. A clerk-typist should be able to type at least three-quarters of a page a minute. And there shouldn't be more than one error a page. So if we keep track of everything they do, then if a clerk-typist meets that average, she should get a rating of 'satisfactory'. A secretary, of course, should do better than that. Say, a page a minute and half an error per page. In order to get a 'commendable' rating, we'll have to factor in some other criteria. I'm working on a list right now and..."

"Ben..."

"Filing, for instance. Do you know that Ginny Jean lost the last draft of my paper? Lost it. Can you imagine..."

"Ben..."

"I had to do all the corrections over again."

"What draft are you on now?"

"Fifteen."

I couldn't keep it up. I laughed.

Ben looked at me blankly for a minute. Then he laughed too. That's the endearing thing about Ben. He thinks he's as nutty as everyone else thinks he is. And yet, the man continues to be a nut.

"Ben, stop this nonsense with grading support staff. It would take all the support staff we've got just to keep the records. You know, you have a convoluted mind."

Ben smiled sweetly. "I know."

"Can you take the United Fund drive?"

"Sure. When does it start?"

"Now. Stevie has the papers."

"Aren't we going to do my performance review now?"

"Yeah. Here's the sheet. Make the numbers come out so you get a 'commendable' and give it back to me for signature. It's Steve's turn for an 'outstanding'. Apart from that, I do want to talk to you about your job. You're driving the support staff up the wall."

"And vice versa."

"Ben, no one else has all that trouble. I'm putting a concrete barrier between you and the typists. When you have something to type, give it to me, tell me how you want it typed, and I'll give it to Ginny Jean. She will give the typing back to me and I'll give it to you. Do not, repeat, do not come within 15 feet of Ginny Jean, starting now and continuing into the foreseeable future."

"Hokay. She was never my type anyway. Listen, Bea, I want to talk to you about something else. I was standing in the reception room a little while ago and I couldn't help overhearing some of the staff meeting." Ben's ears were legendary. "Is Hump really going to RIF me?"

"You don't report to Hump, you report to Don and me."

"Is Hump going to make you RIF me?"

"He can't without RIFfing me first, and he isn't going to do that. He needs me on the Hill. Don't worry, Tschochke, I'll throw my body in front of you. Just stay out of his way."

"Why can't he stand me? What do I do?"

I leaned over the desk and patted Ben on the head. "Some people have less tolerance for pains in the ass than others."

I turned to leave. "Bea," Ben said quietly, "I need this job. There's no place for me to bump to."

"I know that, Tschoch. But lest you think we're carrying you as a charity case, forget it. Strange as you are, we need you. So get to work."

I went back to my office and began thumbing through the Congressional Directory. I didn't know a soul on the Trade and Industry subcommittee. I called Hope Lahti, an old friend of Harry's and mine, who directs the House Science Committee staff. I caught her just as she was about to leave for the staff Christmas party.

"Hope, I need a favor."

"If you're crazy enough to go out with a House staffer, George is getting a divorce."

For one mad moment I considered it. Three years without a man is a helluva long time. But George?

"You still there, Bea?"

"Uh, yeah. Sorry. Not that kind of a favor. Do you know anyone on Trade and Industry?"

"Yep. Gordon Bryce went over from here to be the staff director. Don't you know him?"

"I may have seen him. If so, I didn't know his name."

"He's a good guy even if he does drive his wife nuts. What's wrong?"

"The OMB budget mark is a disaster and I've been named point-person on the Hill."

"Call Gordon. Use my name if you think it will help. I'm going home for Christmas. When I get back, I have to prepare for a hearing on the nineteenth so I can't do anything until then. Call me on the twentieth and we can get together. I'll help you with the strategy if you want. Meanwhile, see if you can think up some sexy headline-grabber demonstration that will get the Members' pictures in their hometown papers. That's usually good for a million or so in the budget."

I thanked Hope, looked up Bryce's number, and dialed. He was in. A new first in Congressional relations.

"Gordon? This is Bea Goode."

"Who?"

"I'm with LIT."

"With who?"

"LIT. The Lab for Industrial Technology."

"Oh. Yeah."

"Hope Lahti thought you might be willing to listen to LIT's problems."

"What's it about?"

"OMB is cutting our budget in half. Looks like a prelude to zeroing us out."

"Jesus. Aren't you the guys who watch the export technologies?"

"That's us."

"So who's going to do that job?"

"You tell me."

"Jesus. Listen, I got to leave for our Christmas party now, but we should talk. Can you come over to the party?"

"Give me fifteen minutes." I grabbed my coat and ran.

The party was taking place in one of the big hearing rooms. Chairs had been moved to one side to make room for tables full of goodies. The majestic platform, on which the magisterial committee members usually sit, remained in place. The room was packed when I got there. Unlike the Executive branch, the Hill has no rule against booze on the premises and everyone looked reasonably well oiled. I knocked on the shoulder of the first person I could reach and asked for Gordon Bryce. The shoulder pointed at a tall, sandy-haired man who looked familiar. I pushed my way through the crowd.

"I'm Bea Goode."

"I think we've met. C'mon into the next office and tell me what it's all about."

I snaffled a cup of punch and followed him out. "I just found out about it this morning. All I know right now is that they've given us a three million mark."

"How much do you have now?"

"Six."

"What do you do with the money? It can't cost all that much to watch exports."

"Not if the exports are dry goods. High-tech is different. First, we have to know, in gross, whether there will be much of an export market for the product in question. If not, it doesn't make sense for the Government to put resources into pushing it. A lot of the countries we might sell to have fairly restrictive import barriers and it's not good policy for us to spend negotiating- credits for something that won't have much impact anyway. Second, it's not enough to know what a product does. We also have to know what its components might be used for. Trade is important, but national security has priority. We have to be sure that we don't export a widget that contains a chip that can be adapted to help the bad guys blow our brains out. The only effective way we can tell what the components can be used for is to work with them in our labs. And labs cost."

Gordon eyed me speculatively. "Are you married?"

"No, but you are. Keep your mind on business and your hands on your punch cup."

"Well, a man can but try.

"Can't you just ask some experts if something is a danger to national security? Run seminars or something?"

"Gordon, we are the experts."

"Jesus. Have they heard your protest yet?"

"No. The appeal isn't until after the holidays."

"What are the chances that OMB will restore?"

"I don't know. We're trying to get a feel for it, but I doubt if there will be enough people around to find out anything until after the first. If I had to guess cold, I'd say 'small chance'. We're too little for the Secretary to notice -- he probably doesn't know we exist -- and he would have to get behind us if we have a hope in hell for the appeal."

"Jesus. O.K. I'll talk to the Chairman but it will have to be after recess. We'll be back on the twelfth. Call me then. Let me warn you, though, even if we do something, you're going to have to convince Appropriations. We propose. They dispose."

"Can you give me any help with them?"

"Maybe. Call me on the fifteenth. Meanwhile, see if you can think up something that will generate a little publicity in the Members' Districts.

"Would you believe me if I told you my wife doesn't understand me?"

"Now why do I think she understands you all too well?'

Bryce shrugged, got up and went back to his party. I went back to LIT and our own party. No booze, but Stevie had made a huge pot of chili with his own two hands and a hot plate. I seldom drink anyway.

About 4:00, I picked up Boobie's file and got my car. The dead man awaited me.

"Harry, I'm working in a squirrel cage. LIT's about to go down the tube, and the only person who can save the nation is me -- me and my vaunted Hill contacts. What Hill contacts? Hope Lahti and three of her staff from an unrelated committee. The odds don't look good. And what is the Director and his staff doing while awaiting the Apocalypse?

"Hooey boy! You can't turn right from that lane, you nutcake." This time a blue Volvo. What is it about Volvos that infect their owners with lunacy? Or maybe only lunatics buy them.

"I'll tell you what they were doing. The Director is off on a boondoggle; the Deputy Director for Operations is sitting on a RIF panel, making sure that no one gets fired before the arrival of the Four Horsemen; the Technical Director is drawing up a five-year plan for the purpose of revising it in four months (a five year plan for God's sake, when we've got five minutes); the Executive Officer is learning to be a programmer; the Senior Economist (I'm pleading with you, don't laugh), while picking her way between a RIF and a bump, is planning to produce a Busby Berkely spectacular

based in a high-tech lab; the Trade Specialist is running around with a tin cup asking for United Fund contributions; the Computer Specialist is playing end-man in a minstrel show; and the Chief Scientist is getting sloshed in her office.

"No. That is not your fender, it's mine.

"Hold it, buster, red means stop.

"You may not know, sweetie, that there are regulations against bureaucrats (that's me) lobbying the Congress. There is a fiction to be maintained, to wit, whatever mark you get from OMB is the position of the Administration, and whatever is the position of the Administration is just and good. It is also bull bleep. When the budget mark is a disaster, the bureaucrats head for the Hill and try to get it reversed. The problem is that if you get caught you get canned. So why me? Does Hump really think I have the contacts to do it? In a pig's eye. It's a question of risk. If Congress sustains the mark, half of LIT gets RIFfed and Hump's between-the-lines threat is that I'm in that half. So, if I can't get the mark reversed, I'm on the street. And if I get caught, I'm on the street. Moral: get the mark reversed and don't get caught."

CHAPTER 3

January 8, 1990

The holiday season was staggering to its conclusion (And, incidentally, the murder season was about to begin). The RIF panel had met and, after due deliberation, officially decided that Boobie could not do my job nor (unofficially) any other. However, they gave him one anyway. God knows whose.

I had no great flashes of insight in re: sexy demonstration. The Members could probably benefit from a sober, lucid exposition on the relationship between high-tech consumer products and instruments of annihilation. Maybe Hump, wearing a fig leaf, could jump out of a cake on the House floor and deliver the lecture. Maybe Hump, not wearing a fig leaf....

Hump returned on January 8, only four days after he was expected. Lenore buzzed me at 10:15 to tell me that I was late for the staff meeting.

"What staff meeting?"

"Mr. Stafford scheduled a meeting at 10:00 with you, Don, and John."

"No one told me. Did you think of telling them?"

"Look, Bea, I can't be expected to do everything. I'm very..."

I hung up and trotted off to Hump's conference room, where John and Don sat glaring at one another. Hump was nowhere in sight. "Where's our leader?"

"He's not here yet."

"Then what was Lenore having such a fit about?"

Don grinned. "Practice, practice, practice."

Hump's paunch preceded him into the room. "Sorry I'm late."

"Did you have a good vacation?" John asked.

"Crappy. I don't know why Mauve thinks that those touchyfeely things are vacations. At least this time we didn't have to run around mother-naked. The only thing we bared were our purses. Well, I guess we're all here. Let's get started." He walked over to the coffee pot and sloshed some in the general vicinity of his cup.

"We might as well start with the new OMB budget analyst. Did Steve find out anything about him?"

"Her," said Don. "Her name is Frieda Langsteth and she comes from the budget office of one of Interior's Bureau of Mines installations out west."

Hump spilled yet more coffee, produced a hankie, and began mopping his pants.

John remarked that there were rumors that she was gay. Hump deposited the rest of his coffee on the floor. He got down on his hands and knees and began mopping. From under the table, his voice asked, "Does anyone know something useful about her? Like how she feels about LIT?"

Silence.

Hump clambered back onto his seat. "Well, we'll find out when she gets here tomorrow. I don't suppose we need any more intelligence on her."

"Did you say 'gets here tomorrow'?" Don was incredulous.

"Yeah. I'm sorry. OMB called just before I left for the TIP meeting and I forgot to tell Lenore to tell you. She's due here..." Hump searched for a piece of paper in his jacket pocket. "...at 10:30. We'd better plan the briefing."

"I can give her the technical briefing." Apparently John expected the lady to be safely ignorant. "Do you want me to greet her in the lobby?"

"Thanks, John. Yeah. You do that."

"Don't you think you ought to greet her?" I asked. "She'll be expecting it."

"No. No. I haven't been here for two weeks and she might ask me something I don't know about. I won't have time to get up to speed before she gets here. I'll give her the welcome talk. Fill something with air for me, Bea."

"Main conference room? Do we want to impress her?"

"Yeah. Do we need anything else?"

Don suggested that we fill her in on the work we're doing for NASA. "It's at least as impressive as the conference room."

"I can include that in the technical briefing," John said.

"Come on, John," Don said. "You can share the limelight with someone who knows something. Alex Carfil is doing the work and he might as well give the briefing."

"Well, maybe." John sounded dubious. "Those engineers aren't too swift."

"And you are, huh?"

"Come on, boys." Hump looked at me. "Bea, tell Carfil he's on tomorrow."

"He'll be thrilled." I didn't know Carfil, but if he was like the other engineers, he was going to have some really rotten words to say about being dragged out of his lab to give a talk he hadn't had time to prepare. "She'll expect lunch. I'll lay it on."

"Do we have to feed her?" Hump sounded plaintive.

"Yes," Don said.

"Well, do I have to be there? I'm on a diet."

"Then just pick at your food, Hump. This is no time to offend the OMB budget analyst."

"Oh, alright," Hump grumped. "Let's get to seating

arrangements."

"I have a swell idea," I said. "Let's all walk into the room and sit down."

"I needed a smart-ass economist. You better sit on one side of the lady. And put Carfil on the other, just in case she's not a dyke."

Laughter.

Hump continued, "I'll sit at the far end of the table so she can't ask me questions I don't know the answer to. I guess we're finished."

"Hump," I said, "the Hill staffers think we should have a demo."

"Save it until after the briefing, Bea."

John, Don, and I walked out together. "Fellas," I said, "can't one of you brief Hump tonight so he can take a more active part in the morrow's festivities?"

John looked at me. "Monday's his poker night."

I walked down one flight to the labs where LIT's techies hang out and began searching for Carfil's room number. As I got close, I heard the warble of an off-key tenor.

My name is John Wellington Wells dee dee boop

I deal in magic and spee-ells

My name is John Wellington, name is John Wellington

The racket was coming from Carfil's lab. I knocked and stuck my head in. The lab had the general appearance of a squirrel's nest, only not as neat. There were piles of debris over every surface, some of which were probably parts of chairs. At least legs were visible underneath the mess. There were also tables, which had more extensive surfaces, higher piles of debris, and fatter legs. There was a window and a window ledge and, no surprise, more debris.

"I'm Beatrice Goode. I need some magic and spells."

"Siddown." He cleared what appeared to be a mound of prophylactic devices off a chair. "Have a cookie."

I couldn't recall having seen Carfil before. He was a tousle-haired man, four or five inches taller than my five foot four. Probably around my age. More adorable-looking than handsome. Sexy in an oblivious way. Dammit, Bea, stop that!

"Here, taste one. I made them. Tell me what you think."

I bit into a chocolate meringue. "Not bad. They could probably stand a few drops of almond flavoring."

"Almond!" Carfil looked outraged. "I knew the minute I saw you that you didn't have a taste bud in your head."

"Then why'd you ask for my opinion?"

"Because I didn't think you'd give me one. You were supposed to say 'Oh, Dr. Carfil, I simply must have the recipe'."

"I'm a brute. Oh, Dr. Carfil, I simply must have the recipe. Now may I have some magic and spells?"

Carfil grinned. He really was adorable. "I've seen you around. Aren't you on Stafford's staff?"

"Uh huh."

"You here for the same reason as Chandler?"

"I don't know why Stevie was here."

"He comes down every once in a while to find out about export control. What makes some things marketable and some things not; what the latest findings are. He's a smart guy. He asks good questions."

"He is a smart guy. The rest of the staff should find out more about LIT's business. Unfortunately, that's not why I'm here."

"Oh?"

"We're going through the budget exercise and the analyst from OMB will be here tomorrow at 10:30. Stafford would like you to brief her on the NASA project then join us for lunch."

"Tomorrow morning?"

"Tomorrow morning."

"For God's sake, are you...O.K., O.K. Have another cookie. Where?"

I bit on another meringue. Maybe he was right about the almond. "The main conference room. You can join us at 11:30. Don't put together a dog-and-pony. Informal. Just give her an honest progress report. But leave out the bad parts."

"Do you know what I think?"

"The same thing that I think. May I have another cookie?"

"Only if you take the recipe, too."

"All engineers are sadists. Alright, I'll take the damn recipe."

"What do you do here?"

"Trivia, mostly. But at a very senior level. My title is Senior Economist."

Carfil looked at me critically. "You don't look like an economist."

"I'm not."

"Then why are you called Senior Economist?"

I munched another meringue. "Because of the way they classify slots. If you're in an identifiable area of esoterica, something that uses formulae or prescriptions, your director tells personnel what specialty is needed and a slot for that specialty is produced -- if you haven't gone over the slot allowance. But since no one knows what a squishy thing like an economist or political scientist or policy analyst does, the personnel department decides what you need. They're not supposed to, but they do. Anyway, Hump and Don decided LIT needed a management scientist and they sent the papers to personnel, from whence it was returned with the opinion that LIT did not need a management scientist. Then Don went to see the personnel director and found out that he would buy off on an economist. So they advertised for an economist, hoping that a management scientist might turn up."

"But how did you get classified as an economist?"

"You have to understand the system. The Office of Personnel Management's classifiers are either kids or burned out cases. Either they don't know anything or they knowitall. They have a list of words that they match to occupations. Among the words that are attached to the occupation 'economist' are 'cost' and 'benefit'. Then they have a list of educational level, work experience, and publications that are attached to grade levels. Follow?"

"Have another cookie."

I bit. "Anyhow, about twelve years ago, I was a grad student in Administration and the man I later married was in grad school in Archaeology. As joke Christmas presents for our friends, we dummied up a publication called *The Journal of Archaeology and Administration* and wrote a spoof called 'Costs and Benefits of Sacrificial Offerings as Practiced in Urly Ur: An Alternative to Modern Taxation Policy'".

"Oh my God," said Carfil.

"It goes on. It turned out to be a very popular Christmas present, and we issued a new edition of The Journal and wrote a new cost benefit analysis every year. Last year, I got bored with the job I had, and decided that it would probably be a good thing if I stopped theorizing for a while and actually tried to practice my trade. So I filled out one of those crazy OPM forms and, just to see what would happen, I included those cost-bennies in the publications section. Well, they saw all those publications, and all that schooling, and all that work experience..."

"And classified you as a Senior Economist."

"You've got it. Don couldn't believe it when a management scientist walked in."

"So you really do management science here."

"No. I write speeches. Why don't we finish the cookies then you and I can meet Don for lunch."

"Desert first? That sounds like the way you guys would do it. O.K."

He bent down, scooped up the prophylactic devices, and deposited them on the chair. "Upsy daisy, Tarzan."

"Tarzan?"

"The swingin' robot."

"That mess of cables is a robot?"

"You were expecting Star Trek?" He scowled at the cables. "Make it so, Tarzan."

I giggled. He took pity on me. "The cables are attached to the computer, which sends out commands and then the cables do what they're told."

"Can you program them to do anything?"

"Don't get bawdy, lady."

Don and Alex and I headed off across the mall, dodging the shin-splinted zanies who think it's healthy to run around in their underwear in January. We made it to the Smithsonian's residents lounge, joined the cafeteria line, and brought our roast beef to a table. "Hump's got himself on an interagency committee on export control." Don signaled the drinks waiter and we got our coffee. "Hump's the technical rep."

"Stafford? He's a software guy -- and out of date at that."

"Well, it's not too bad. The membership list came into the office this morning and I got a peek at it. It's a strange committee. There are a lot of industry guys on it. And they're from a funny level. There aren't many technical people there. Upper middle management, mostly. Looks like the companies are worried about the trade implications and don't want to trust the export decisions to their tech staff. If we're gonna hold our own, it'll have to be someone like Hump or me. I guess they're all doing what we're doing. Getting their management briefed enough to understand the general technology and putting the discussion at the policy level.

"The other funny thing about the membership list is that Hump's the only guy with a software background on it. So we'll probably have the final word on software."

"Does he know enough?"

"Well, he's rusty, but he used to be one of the artificial intelligence stars at P-Sof before he went to DoD, so he'll do o.k."

"What about that other guy from your office who comes snooping around -- can he back Stafford up?"

"Stevie?" I asked. "He's the exec officer."

"No, not him. He's smarter than this guy. An older guy with a hick accent who says he runs the place."

"Lee Roy," Don and I said.

"Yeah, him. Can he back up Stafford?"

Don crunched his pickle. "Lee Roy couldn't back up a Chevvie. What's he snooping around about?"

"I dunno. He asks the damndest questions. He asked me if I was a Montygoo or a Capaletti."

"Huh?"

"That's what I said. He said there was some kind of conspiracy going on in the Director's office, and he wanted to know whose side the tech staff is on."

"Who's supposed to be conspiring to do what?"

"I don't know, exactly. He hemmed, hawed, and hinted that some unnamed people were trying to unseat Stafford and that, while he (Lee Roy) would certainly be appointed to take Stafford's place if that happened, he had no ambitions. Said he was just trying to find out how bad things were."

"I suppose I've heard crazier things," said Don, "but I can't remember any right now. Is there anything going on that you know about?"

"No. Are you guys Montygoos or Capalettis?"

"Bea's a Gemini," Don said.

"I wonder how Lee Roy knew about Montagues and Capulets," I mused.

Don laughed. "They did a revival of West Side Story on TV a few weeks ago and they told about where it came from."

"Listen," Alex said, "as long as we're discussing conspiracies in your office, was there some dark plot behind your waiting until today to ask me to make a presentation tomorrow?"

"Don't ask," said Don. "Hump got the date just before he went on vacation and forgot to give it to us. Bea went down to see you as soon as we found out."

"That's some Director you've -- we've got. Do I see cause for conspiracy?"

"Naw. Hump's O.K. It's his wife."

"She forgot to tell you?"

I laughed. "Hump's married to a putative sex-pot who decides at frequent, but irregular intervals, that Hump is working himself to a shadow. So Mauve starts instigating for a vacation, Hump finds himself a boondoggle, and the two of them drop off the face of the earth for a week or two. She gets involved with every fad that comes along and they usually wind up some bizarre place. This time they went on an EST retreat."

Alex waved at the drinks waiter, who ignored him. "Maybe he can't get it up in Washington. Sorry, Bea."

"Why should you be sorry?" I asked, "You don't even know the guy. I am now going to change the subject. How's the Tarzan project going?"

"Frustratingly. I'm trying to get the two arms to work together. There's a glitch that's been bugging me for the last week. I think I'm close now. I could have done without that presentation tomorrow."

"What's the problem?" Don asked.

"For the first functionality demonstration," Alex explained, "Tarzan's arms are supposed to twist a cap off of a jar. When the cap is loose enough, the tactile sensors are supposed to signal that it's time to stop twisting and to start lifting. Something's not working and the arms just go on a-twisting. I wasn't sure whether it was the sensors or the program, but I think I've finally got it isolated in the program. It's been a bitch."

Thoughts of sexy demonstrations danced in my head. "Alex," I innocently asked, "when will Tarzan be ready for demonstration?"

"Never, if I don't get back to work."

Alex went back to his lab. No doubt about it; he was the most adorable man I'd come across since Harry died.

Don and I continued up to the fifth floor. "Don, does Lee Roy actually think there's some kind of cabal?"

Don shrugged. "It's more likely he's trying to start one and he thinks he's being smart about it. The jerk really believes he's gonna be the next director."

I dropped off at my office, sat down at the micro, and began to fill Hump's welcoming talk with air. Ben came in,resplendent in taupe polyester. "I thought I heard you. Do you know what Ginny Jean did this time? She lost two whole tables of statistics! Bea, I'm going to sign up for a word processing course so I can type my own manuscripts and I won't have to depend on that idiot. It would be a lot more useful than Ada and..."

"Ben. Two points. First, I put you in for a word processing course two months ago and Personnel sent the application back with a note saying it was 'inappropriate for a GS13 to take word processing'. So unless you are willing to take a grade reduction, forget it. Second, I told you to stay away from Ginny Jean, to eschew her company, to bug off. Why-"

"Oh. I thought you meant on future manuscripts. She already had the statistics and I just wanted..."

"I'll get your statistics, Ben. Just sit down and wait for me here. Do not move."

Ben sat and I walked down to the office Ginny Jean shared with two other clerk-typists. Ginny Jean's printer was clicking away. "Ginny Jean, where are Ben's statistics?"

Ginny Jean looked up. "I'm printing them out now, Bea."

"Why didn't you print them out when Ben asked for them?"

"Well, I couldn't. He was looking over my shoulder."

I walked over and looked at her file folder. It was labeled "NUTCASE4."

"Ginny Jean, rename the file to something that is both inoffensive and reminds you of Ben. And if Ben asks you for anything else, refer him to me."

One of the other clerks giggled. "Impossible. There is nothing inoffensive that would remind us of Ben."

I waited for the print-out and brought it back to my office. Ben was reading the material on my screen. "Is this Hump's welcome speech for the OMB analyst?"

"Yeah."

"Won't he stumble over 'synergy'? He's not going to have time to practice, you know."

I looked at the screen. "You're right. 'Interaction'?"

"Better. Not perfect, but better."

I handed him the print-out. "Here are your statistics. Now get out of here while I finish pumping air."

Ben looked at his newly-printed tables. "Well, I guess she had my number after all."

He left.

I inched the car out of the lot and crept toward the bridge. "*Harry, I've just met an adorable man. An attractive, sexy man and I feel like I'm in the first bloom of adolescence.*

Ridiculous at my age. Maybe I just want to get laid.

It doesn't seem right talking it over with you, but who else have I got? If I hadn't been such a jackass I'd have kept in touch with your Aunt Bessie. The lord knows I love the woman. I just couldn't talk to anyone. And after three years I can hardly call her up and say 'Remember me?' Washington is a funny place. I've got dozens of friends and no one to talk

to. We're all so terribly busy. Not quite true; I can talk to Don about most things. But not about this. Dammit, I don't need Alex to complicate my life right now. And we both know what Bessie would say to that. She'd say 'Yes you do'. That's what she'd say."

I reached over and turned on the radio. Bare Naked Ladies was singing "One Week". Don't even think it, Bea.

CHAPTER 4

January 9, 1990

I xeroxed a couple of copies of Hump's welcome speech and dropped one off with Lenore. "If Hump stops in the office before he goes to the conference room, would you give him this to look over?"

Lenore took the manuscript without comment, and I continued on to the conference room. Don was already there. I put the other copy of the speech at the head of the table and sat down next to him.

"I told Alex to come up at 11:30. It should take John and Hump about an hour to get through their pieces. There's no point in dragging Alex out of his lab to sit through the puff."

Don nodded. "He'd probably throw up and spoil the whole thing anyway. Did you set up lunch?"

"12:30."

Don started to thumb through the speech. "What's with this demonstration you keep hinting about?"

I explained about Hope's and Bryce's advice for a sexy headline-grabber. "The only sexy thing I can think of is Alex."

Don looked at me. "No shit?"

"Let me rephrase that. The only sexy thing I can think of is Alex's robot. Can we plan something around that?"

Don shook his head. "You can talk to him but don't push it. And don't bring it up in the staff meeting. Those software problems can be cleared up in a day or in a year, and there's no way to tell in advance which it'll be. If some dodo like Delamain gets hold of it he'll try to rush the thing into a demo before it's ready. If it fails in the middle of a demo, we're dead. Just remember that NASA disaster a few years back when the political types shoved the spacecraft up when it wasn't fit to fly."

"Yeah. But Tarzan isn't likely to kill anyone."

"Except our budget. Congress couldn't back off of the space program when the bird went down. There were too many heroes involved. But if we screw up there won't be any heroes."

I nodded.

At 10:40, Delamain escorted the OMB analyst into the room. Still no Hump.

Langsteth was a stocky woman, fiftyish, her short, dark hair beginning to go gray. She had a perfectly round face, like Charlie Brown's. Surprising eyes -- gray, deep-set, dreamy. "Ms. Langsteth," John said, "this is Mr. Cromarty, our Director of Operations, and Dr. Goode, our very capable Senior Economist. Sit down right here, Frieda." John placed the analyst at the foot of the table and looked around a little wildly.

"Mr. Stafford has been unavoidably detained," I said. "He'll be here any minute. Are you new to Washington, Ms. Langsteth?"

"Yes." Langsteth fished a notebook from her briefcase, opened it, and glared tight-lipped at the empty place at the head of the table. We held that tableau for a few minutes.

Finally, John said, "Well, maybe I'd better start the technical briefing and Mr Stafford can welcome you, um, when he gets here." John began sorting through a stack of reports.

"My God," I whispered to Don, "that ass is going to push the excretions from his turkey farm."

"Shut up," Don whispered back. "She probably doesn't know enough to ask questions."

"Fat chance."

"Perhaps I should tell you a little bit about LIT first," John said.

"Perhaps Mr. Stafford should do that," Langsteth snapped.

"Oh. Yes. Of course. Uh, yes. Well, I'll get right into the technical briefing, then. LIT prides itself on actually doing things and I have here some of the reports we have produced in the one short year we have been in existence. This one," John held up a slim, dun-colored pamphlet, "is..."

Hump came in. "Sorry I'm late." He took his place at the head of the table. "That damn dog keeps slipping her head out of the collar." He picked up his speech. "Is this my talk?"

"Mr. Stafford," said John, "I'd like you to meet Frieda Langsteth."

Hump nodded. Langsteth nodded. Hump cleared his throat and began to read. He stumbled over 'interaction'. "And now, I think John can fill you in on what our technical staff does with its time."

"Yes," John said. "Before picking up where I left off, I guess I should talk a little about our relationship with OMB itself. As you know, our major mission -- but by no means our only one -- is to patrol the high-tech export waters for the United States Government. But we have a very special relationship with OMB. Our staff consists of some of the best technical people within the government, and we manage to help many of the agencies -- particularly OMB and sometimes even the Congress -- out with their own problems. Did you know, for instance, that it was the LIT staff that advised OMB on its office automation?"

Langsteth lit a cigarette, looked around for an ashtray, shrugged, and put the match in her coffee cup. "Yeah. I wondered about that. Why the hell did you guys do that? I thought that's what GSA was for."

John smiled smugly. "Well, OMB is too important to trust to GSA. OMB felt it needed the best."

"Oh? It looked to me like a straightforward office automation project. Did we ask you to do it or did you volunteer."

"We volunteered. Always helpful."

"And how many man-years did it take?"

"Person-years, Frieda. We're not chauvinists here, you know. About half a person-year."

"That's about $50K?" Langsteth made a note on her pad. I looked over; it said '-50.' "And you did the same for some Congressional committees?"

"Oh, yes," said John happily. "Even for Gov. Ops. That's OMB's authorization committee, you know."

"How many man-years in the Congress?"

"Oh, about the same, overall."

Langsteth subtracted another $50K.

“Well,” said John, “now let me pick up where I left off when Mr. Stafford came in.” He waver the dun-colored report. "We did this for the Department of the Interior. The Bureau of Mines has become a very high-tech operation, and they asked us to do a survey of all the relevant state-of-the-automation-art developments. That, of course, is right in line with our mission and so we..."

"Did they pay you for it?"

"Oh, yes. With our little budget, we could never do all the things we have to do if we didn't supplement the money with some interagency funds. When Alex gets here later, he'll report on the project he's doing with some of the money I got him from NASA. Anyway, to get back to this survey..."

"That report is in a tan cover. I thought the Government Printing Office published in white?"

"GPO didn't publish this. They only publish things of general interest. This is much too specialized."

Langsteth made another note. She covered it up before I could look. "I thought I saw a LIT state-of-the-automation-art survey published by GPO."

"That's a different one, Ms. Langsteth," I said. "My group did that one, and it was for a much wider audience."

"Mmph. Well, who did publish that thing Delamain's waving?"

"We published it ourselves," John said proudly. "That's one of the things we spend our money on."

"Why didn't the Bureau of Mines publish? Wasn't it acceptable?"

Don covered his eyes.

"Oh, they accepted it," John said. "They just didn't think it had wide enough interest to publish."

"And you did. The rest of that pile of...ah...reports you have there. They're all tan covers. Are they all...ah...too 'specialized' for general interest?"

"Well, yes. We are very high-tech."

"How many of them are there?"

"Let's see." John counted. "Eleven. We do a lot of work here."

"And how much does each publication cost you -- just for the publishing."

"Oh. For a hundred page report, about $10K."

"Do the interagency funds cover printing?"

"No."

"So that pile cost LIT about $110K?"

"Plus or minus 10%."

Langsteth made another note. I didn't want to look.

The door opened and Alex slipped into the seat next to Don. It was 11:25.

"John," I said, "Dr. Carfil is here. Perhaps we should interrupt your briefing and let him start his presentation so he can get back to his lab."

"That's O.K.," said Alex. "I'm a little ear..." Don kicked him.

"Sure," said Alex. He grinned at Langsteth. "We're working on two-armed robots for NASA. First, let me tell you what the problem is then I'll tell you where we are in our research.

"The problem we're trying to solve is the repair of satellites in space. As it stands now, if a single key component of a satellite fails, the whole shebang may have to be replaced. There's some redundancy built in, and while that helps, it isn't a total solution. For instance, if we want to replace a communications satellite in orbit, we either have to launch an unmanned rocket or take up a big part of a shuttle-load. Either way, we're out a lot of money -- spent on hardware or lost in shuttle-load revenues. What we'd like to do is send out a single robot repair vehicle, an RRV, capable of visiting and repairing a number of satellites on one trip. To make economic sense, it has to be a robot."

Langsteth stared at him. "Are you telling me that LIT is designing the whole RRV?"

Alex threw up his arms. "Not on your life! An agency

this size couldn't possibly handle that big a job. We're just working on the technology of two-armed manipulation -- other folk are tackling other problems."

Langsteth scribbled some notes. "What's so important about having the two arms?"

Alex beamed. "I thought you'd never ask. For most industrial type tasks, like assembly, one arm is enough. If you think about it, you'll realize that if you're combining a series of parts in a specified way, you only need one arm. Here, look."

Alex picked up Langsteth's pack of cigarettes and removed one. "Suppose my task is to put this cigarette back in the pack. I'm going to use one hand to hold the pack and the other hand to manipulate the cigarette. Like so."

Alex stuffed the cigarette against the pack and broke off the end. "Oh, shit."

Langsteth burst out laughing. "Some robots work better than others. I've got the idea, go on."

Alex grinned. "I guess that needs more work. Anyway, in a factory, something like a specialized 'jig' replaces the arm that holds the thing and the manipulating hand is replaced by a robot.

"Our two-armed robot is really a combination of the 'jig'

and the manipulator. The 'space jig' part will hold the satellite and the manipulator will do the repairs. It's kind of a funny looking thing. The 'jig' part is a telescoping arm with a hand-like set of grippers on the far end. The manipulator is a jointed arm with a three-fingered hand on the end. Between the arm and the hand, there's a camera. Here's a rough sketch."

Langsteth studied the diagram. "Is there anything new in all this?"

"Many, many important things." Delamain grabbed his opportunity by throat. "Of course, it's hard for the layperson to..."

"Not really," said Alex. "The manipulator technology is pretty old. There are a few new wrinkles that take the space environment into account -- like special lubricants that won't freeze solid or evaporate. Most of the hard part has to do with the sensors and the software.

"Getting the arms synchronized has been a bitch. You get a real high-tech collision if the arms bang into one another. You have to remember that the point of this whole thing is to fix satellites, not clobber them, so certain kinds of motions have to be forbidden. You can't build those prohibitions into the hardware, though, because the satellites come in so many different sizes and shapes. So it's a software problem."

"Alex," I cut in, "can't the information about each satellite be sent up from earth when it's being repaired?"

"Sure. But you can't rely on that altogether. That's why you need a vision capability. A camera of some sort. What if we had to try to repair, or capture, a satellite belonging to another country? Where's the information going to come from?"

Langsteth made a few more notes. "Can you sum up the problems for me, Alex?"

"Yeah. The current problems are in coordination and in the interpretation of the information the sensors report. Vision is only one sensory capability. The robot will also have pressure and motion sensors that function like our sense of touch. So the software has to include a set of totally consistent, comprehensive rules for deciding, in any given situation, what the information means and what actions to take. Easy, it ain't."

Langsteth looked bemused. "And all this to repair some satellites?"

"Naw," Don said. "aside from the use they may have in a space vehicle, if we can get this thing working, the spin-offs will knock your socks off. The satellite repair business alone could have some real impact on the balance of trade. But sophisticated space robots would give us a big jump over the world competition in using space to produce a lot of high-tech products. Pharmaceuticals, for instance can be made better in a vacuum, and space is one helluva vacuum. Plain, old earth-bound construction is another area that'll be affected. We get that automated, and we can build all those bridges and tunnels and sewers that we keep putting off because we can't afford it."

Langsteth continued to scribble. "And do you think the construction unions will go along with that, Dr. Goode?"

"Not certain. Provisionally, yes. If this were the sixties or seventies, there would be no hope. But both the unions and management may have learned their lessons. Alex's work could make a difference."

"We should have had all those bastards up for treason in the seventies." This was one of the subjects that pushed Don's button. "I mean it. They were protecting their damned bonuses and stock options and seniority and they didn't give a damn about their country -- or even their kids' future. At least some of those guys must have known they were shooting their country down the tube."

Alex was entranced. "You mean the fate of the nation depends on whether I can get my program de-bugged?"

"We're counting on you, boy," I said.

John cleared his throat. "Interesting as all this is," John said, "I think we should get back to the subject."

"I thought this was the subject," said Langsteth, then to Alex, "Where are you in your research?"

"Hit a real mother of a problem last week. But I think we're moving again. We've got the arms coordinated for some of the gross movements, but the finer tasks are being stubborn."

Langsteth looked absently for the ashtray, shrugged, and put her cigarette out in her cup. "Is it a feedback problem?"

"Sort of. Come down to the lab after lunch and I'll show you what's happening."

"I can't, I've got another meeting scheduled." She looked honestly regretful. "Maybe next week."

"Be sure you schedule it through Mr. Stafford's office," John said.

Alex winked at Langsteth.

Hump rose. "Let's get lunch."

We picked up our food at the Senior Executive Buffet and carried it into one of the private dining rooms. Alex and Langsteth sat down together, engrossed in feedback mechanisms. I sat on Langsteth's other side, Delamain beside me. Don provided an additional buffer between Langsteth and Hump. There were two empty places at the table.

"Well," John said to me, "I think it went very well. She was certainly very interested in how we get our publications out and who reads them. You shouldn't have interrupted me."

I put a forkful of rice into my mouth.

"Yes," he went on, "that was the right presentation. I didn't want her to think we only did the popular-science stuff that your group puts out."

I followed the rice with a chunk of meat. Beef, I think.

"That isn't to say your group doesn't do good work. It's just that she might have wondered if we did any real science. But I wonder about the wisdom of letting Carfil have so much time with her without monitoring. He's talking too much about problems. I don't know how she'll interpret reports of difficulties in the lab."

"You're absolutely right, John. I'd better monitor their conversation." I swiveled toward Langsteth and Alex, blocking Delamain out of the conversation.

Langsteth was saying, "...but I don't understand how you've gotten this far when NASA only came through a month ago."

Alex grinned. "I started this work a few years ago when I was at NASA. Don recruited me when LIT was gearing up and one of the conditions I had for coming here was a lab and some Director's Reserve money to run it. For the first six months we mostly were operating on that. Then Delamain told me that he was going to recommend that some of my funds get transferred to a new videotex project, so I called my former boss at NASA and got the interagency funds. What I'm saying, is that we didn't start from scratch."

"It's impressive, anyway. Can you use more money?"

"Sure. Not too much though." Alex looked over at me. "Don't listen to this, Bea , you'll have a heart attack."

"I'm indestructible." I smiled at Langsteth. "Alex thinks that the only words out of the Director's office are 'Gimme money'."

"Aren't they?" Coldly.

"Only officially. Lunch is free time. And during lunch I'm free to admit that I support Alex on this. He should have enough funds to add a couple of technicians to the project. At this point, I think more professionals would get in the way. Equipment isn't a problem -- we can buy it out of the Special Equipment Fund."

Langsteth looked at Alex. "Is that right?"

"Yeah. And may I say that I am surprised and gratified, Mrs. Goode, that the Director's office understands the situation." Alex looked appropriately surprised and gratified.

"It's too bad the Director himself doesn't," said Langsteth.

Alex looked at his watch. "Would it be o.k. if I cut out, Bea? I should get back to the lab."

"Unless Ms. Langsteth has more questions, it's o.k. with me."

Langsteth shook her head and Alex decamped.

She lit a cigarette while I rummaged around in the sideboard for an ashtray.

"Does LIT have any more guys like him?"

I laughed. "I don't think the world has any more guys like Alex. But we do have a strong technical staff. If you sneak over next week, I'll give you a tour. Don't make it official or you'll get Delamain again."

"Christ." Langsteth shuddered. "Everyone calls me Freddy. And in answer to your previously ignored question, yes, I'm new to Washington. Came from one of those 'high-tech' Bureau of Mines labs that Delamain was yapping about. BoM budget office. In Cupertino. How long have you been here?"

"About 15 years. I was a grad student at Johns Hopkins. I've only been a Fed for a year, though."

"Probably why you sound human. What made you join the zoo?"

"Restlessness, mostly. My husband died, and I just didn't want to keep on doing what I had been doing. Not a rational decision, but I don't regret it."

Freddy swallowed some coffee. "Know what you mean. Got divorced about five years ago and had the same feeling. Took almost five years to do something about it, though." She stubbed out her cigarette. "Why the hell am I telling you this? Never talk about it."

"I suppose it beats bitching to the cat."

We both laughed.

Hump got up. "Well, I suppose we had all better get back to work. I'm sure Ms. Langsteth has things to do, even if we don't."

The rest of the day passed routinely. I sat in on an export briefing, had a slanging match with DoTI's budget office, re-hashed Langsteth's visit with Don, who was trying to make up his mind whether to slash his wrists or cut Delamain's throat, and stuck my head into Alex's lab to give him a thumbs-up sign and get an apricot ice box cookie.

At 5:00, I looked through the accumulated stack of official documents on my desk. Among them were the Announcements of DoTI awards. Hump was getting a gold for 'excellence in management'. I choked. Ballsap and Wenter were getting a bronze for 'technical accomplishment'. I threw the pile in the wastebasket and went down for my car.

The radio was playing the March from 'The Love of Three Oranges' as I drove over the bridge. "*Harry,*" *I said,* "*we have completed our migration through the looking glass. Hump, who has managed us into any number of paper bags, but who has yet to learn how to manage us out of one, is about to receive a gold medal and $45K for managerial excellence. And two of Delamain's prize turkeys are getting bronzes. And do you know what for? For a cut-and-paste, state-of-the-automation-art survey they did for the Bureau of Mines. A survey that the BoM accepted under protest and refused to publish. Ees dees a seestem?*

"Love, what am I gonna do about Alex? He thinks I'm a happily married woman. Or at least a married woman. I'm afraid to tell him I'm not. What if he makes a casual pass? What do I do then? Worse, what do I do if he doesn't make a pass? Jump his bod?"

I turned up the radio's volume and drove home, musing about Alex. Was I falling in love or was it just plain lust? Damned if I could tell the difference. I took a cold shower before I went to bed.

March 9, 1990

...Unnoticed by the multitude, Alex made an 'aw, it was nuthin' gesture. He really was cute.

Now the arms swung toward their next task - the stool. Abruptly, they paused, changed direction, and accelerated toward the figure standing at the edge of the roof.

I closed my eyes. Opened them again. *Oh, my God, no! Stop!*

At the computer terminal, Alex frantically punched at the keys. But Tarzan had reached his destination. The little robot arm unflexed and pushed.

CHAPTER 5

February 13, 1990

I walked into Stevie's office early Tuesday morning. He was on the phone. He motioned at me to sit down and mouthed, "My broker."

"It's a lock, I tell ya," he said into the phone. "They're gonna make a bundle. Buy me another hundred. Yeah. Gi' my love to Cleo, and tell her I'll be up over the weekend." He hung up.

"He's my cousin. Hey, Bea, you in the market for some disks?"

"Floppies?"

"Yeh." Steve reached behind him and grabbed a handful of bright orange-colored disks. He held one out to me. It was labeled 'Bittybyte'. How cute. "High density. I can get all the boxes you want for a sawbuck each."

"The price is right, Steve, but I've never heard of the brand. Are you sure they won't swallow the data?"

"Naw. I've used a few of them and they're o.k. The company went bankrupt, and my brother bought up the whole stock. Besides, they're guaranteed."

"Who guarantees the product of a bankrupt company?"

Steve laughed. "Pick, pick, pick. You want some or not?"

"Thanks, but I guess not. Keep them out of the office, will you? I can just hear Ben if Ginny Jean's disks get wiped out."

Steve howled. "I gotta admit, you got a point. Sure you don't want some for home?"

"Thanks, but no. I don't use enough of them to make it worth your trouble. Did you find out anything about the OMB budget mark?"

"Yeh. I talked to Andy in the DoTI budget office. They're Washington Monumenting us."

"Oh, rats!"

'The Washington Monument' is the Executive's most venerable budget ploy, surfacing whenever austerity is mentioned. It was conceived decades ago by a bureaucratic genius in the Park Service. The Service, hit with a budget cut, saved a bit on its utility bill by shutting down the elevators of the Washington Monument, thereby forcing thousands of visitors to hike up to the top of the structure (the staircase was still in use then). Particularly during D.C.'s muggy summers, this was a hardship that very few of the visitors were willing to let pass unremarked. And they remarked it very forcefully indeed to their elected Representatives on the Hill. The

Hill swiftly restored the Service's budget and 'Washington Monumenting' nearly as swiftly became part of every budget officer's arsenal.

"What makes them think we're a Monument? If they offer us up, the Hill will take us."

"I know," Steve said. "But they gotta come up with something, and they think we can convince the Hill that we're crucial to trade."

"Those bozos! The fact that we're crucial to trade doesn't mean that we can convince the Hill. Dammit!"

Stevie shrugged. "Sorry, Bea. There's no way they'll change their minds. I argued with Andy for half an hour. He wouldn't budge. And it wouldn't have made any difference if he did. The Assistant Secretary made the decision."

I sat there glumly trying to think of some way to explain to Alex why his lab wasn't as important as the elevator in the Washington Monument.

"Bea, is there something else I can do?"

"No, Steve, thanks."

"I'll pick up some of your administrative crap, if you want. It'll give you more time to hit the Hill."

"Be careful. I may take you up on that."

Steve walked around the desk and patted my shoulder. "You and Don'll get it done. LIT's too important to go under. How're you doing on the Hill?"

"Dunno. The subcommittee's staff director was certainly receptive, but they just got back from recess. I'll know more tomorrow. I don't have a line to the Senate at all. Rats! Well, what else is new, kiddo?"

Steve walked back to his desk and sat down, gingerly. Skinny pants are not conducive to free movement.

"OPM is doing an audit on Frances."

"Oh, dear."

Frances Monk was LIT's Chief Scientist. She was a lush. Out of curiosity, I had looked up her career and found it to be a distinguished one. In the mid-seventies, she had become interested in data base management and, with a few research assistants, had developed the architecture that formed the basis of almost every data base management system in current use. Librarians, investment managers, political campaigners, social scientists, the army, navy, air force and marines -- everyone who uses a computer to store very large files -- owes a debt to Frances Monk. But she did all of that before she pickled her brain. She was now a specter who spent her days in a locked office getting quietly sozzled. She kept a bottle stashed in her classified safe.

"I don't understand why we don't RIF her and give her an early retirement," Steve said.

"She'll bump someone we need, Stevie. You want Frances to do the software for the 2-armed robot? Tarzan can do without a pickled brain."

"But she's old enough to take the early out."

"Yeah, but she doesn't have enough years in to get a pension big enough to live on. She's only been a Fed for ten years. She was an academic until then."

"Then why don't we just fire her for being a drunk?"

"Couple of reasons. The one I like is that the country owes her something. She never did get the academic standing she deserved -- by the time the women's movement got around to the universities, she was too long in the tooth to benefit. The young loud-mouths got all the plums. But we're still living off her contributions. We owe her."

Steve looked skeptical. "What's the other reason."

"We can't fire her. Hump investigated. Turns out that you have to send your drunks for counseling, and only if, after six months, the problem hasn't gone away, can you dismiss for cause. And then it's appealable to the Merit System."

"You mean it takes at least six months to fire a stew bum?"

"You got it. It was almost worse."

"No kidding."

"Some years ago, the American Medical Association declared that alcoholism was a disease. Now, as you have no doubt noticed, we are supposed to give hiring and retention preference to the handicapped. Well, about six years back, one of the regulation writers at OPM decided that 'disease' was synonymous with 'handicap' and..."

"I don't wanna hear this," Steve said.

"It's o.k. Reason prevailed. They circulated the draft regulation, and there was enough of an uproar to make them withdraw it. But we came close to preferring drunks."

Ben, in chartreuse day-glo tie, stuck his head through the interconnecting door. "I prefer blondes, myself. Talking about Frances?"

"Just finishing."

"Would either of you care to contribute to the United Fund?"

"Sure," said Steve. "Put me down for fifty."

"Bea?"

"Not a nickel. Have you seen their headquarters over in Alexandria? I'm damned if I'm going to pay to water an atrium."

"C'mon, Bea," Steve said. "You gotta contribute to charity."

"I do. I bought $1,000 worth of warm clothes at Woody's sale and sent it to the Salvation Army. It's the only way I can be sure my contribution goes to someone who needs it."

"Hell," said Ben. "We're not going to make our quota. Hump, at least, contributed a buck. That way I can count him."

"That cheap bastard," Steve said. "Or does he contribute someplace else, too?"

"No, he told me that his alimony's draining him dry."

I got up. "Back to the mill." I walked to my office whistling, 'Please Don't Talk About Me, When I've Gone.'

I looked out of my window, across Independence Avenue, at the wonderful relic that was The Smithsonian's Arts and Industry Building. It was one of those incongruously balmy days that Washington sometimes gets in mid-winter, and the building had a springtime, festive look with the sun glinting off its colorful façade. The gothic hulk of the Castle loomed off to the left, behind the Sackler Gallery of Middle Eastern Studies. What a time that had been for Washington architecture! The Renwick was built in the same era and, I think, the Old Executive Office Building and probably the Patent Court. For sheer ebullience, I can't think of any period, anywhere, to match it. A magnificent city and, despite its looniness, one that was built to last -- at least in the important respects. Not too unlike the Nation.

The roar of an airplane, passing over the building, interrupted my reveries.

I stopped window-gazing and approached my computer table, bending down to retrieve the notes I had stowed on the little recessed shelf. As usual, I clunked my head on the way up and, as usual, vowed not to stow things there anymore. I was still rubbing the bump when there was a tentative knock on the door. "Come in."

A small, sunken-cheeked man, with a wispy beard and a glazed look entered. He looked vaguely familiar.

A very familiar bass rumble said, "Got a few minutes, Bea?"

"Gus! Good heavens, what's happened?"

Augustus Schnabel lowered himself into my visitor's chair.

The last time I had seen Gus, about two months ago, he had been sloppily overweight, grossly self-satisfied, impossibly arrogant, and I liked him. He was regarded - without dissent, so far as I knew -- as the best software person in LIT. Gus was a natural teacher and whenever my lack of technical knowledge got in my way, I would beetle down to Gus's office and humbly ask for instruction. Gus always obliged and, despite his accustomed arrogance, never made me feel like the fool I was. It must have been late last November when I beetled down for a tutorial and found his door locked. When I asked, Delamain told me that Gus was on leave. Apart from feeling mildly affronted by his sneaking off without letting me know, I didn't think much more about it.

"Look at me, Bea. I haven't been able to keep anything on my stomach since this thing started. I've lost over 50 pounds and still counting. I'm sedated all the time because if I'm not I cry. You don't have any idea what it's like to cry all the time. We've been friends, Bea. Will you tell them to drop it?"

I was totally dumfounded. "What are you talking about, Gus?"

"We've been friends, Bea. Don't crap with me."

I finally convinced Gus to tell me the story. It was ugly. Gus had been using the LIT computer as a tool in his private investment management business. He had loaded the holdings of over 100 clients onto the central computer and had used our data management and analysis tools to service the accounts. According to Gus, our equipment had served his clients very well -- they were averaging a 17% higher return on assets than the clients of the top ten investment management firms. Great.

Then came the computer scandal at the Morfant Labs, where some of the computer scientists had been caught using the government machine to handicap the ponies. Apparently, the resulting brouhaha had caused Hump to do a sweep of our central system and lo! Gus got caught.

Hump turned the mess over to the Inspector General who, with Hump's agreement, caused criminal proceedings to be instituted. Gus was in grave danger of going to jail.

"If I had had any sense," said Gus, "I'd have put it in a classified account. They'd never have caught me."

"If you had had any sense, you nincompoop, you wouldn't have done it at all."

"It wasn't doing any harm -- the machine is under-utilized. Are you going to tell them to drop it?"

"This is the first I've heard of it, Gus. If they didn't see fit to tell me about it in the first place, I doubt if they'll see fit to drop it on my say-so. But yes, I'll try."

The little shrunken man got up and walked to the door. "You know what, Bea? I don't believe a fucking word you said." He closed the door gently.

I thought about it for a bit, and by the time I was finished thinking, I was thoroughly angry at everyone. Gus, Don, Hump, everyone. I decided to beard Don first.

He was on the phone arranging his softball schedule when I reached his office. He finished the conversation and asked, "What's up?"

"I just saw Gus Schnabel."

"I didn't know he was back from leave. Carfil must be glad to see him!"

I stared at Don. "Then you weren't told, either."

"Huh?"

I unfolded the story of Gus's ruination.

"I don't believe it. Hump would never do something like that on his own." Don got up. "C'mon."

The two of us marched past a startled Lenore and Don banged on Hump's door.

"Yo!"

Don and I walked in to find Hump and Lee Roy huddled over the micro screen. "Hi, Clyde, LuLuBelle." Lee Roy turned back to the screen. "Have you been down in that quarry yet, Hump? That might do something."

Hump considered, shook his head. "Too dangerous. Bad things could happen."

Those two fools were playing 'Adventure'.

"Goddammit," said Don and I.

Hump chuckled and got up. "Are you going to give a unison performance or is Bea scheduled for the descant?"

Don said, "Gus Schnabel just left Bea's office."

Hump shook his head sorrowfully. "That. God, that was the hardest thing I've ever had to do. Couldn't sleep well for a week. But it had to be done. It had to be done."

Don's face was getting red. "Why? And why in hell did you do it without talking it over with the staff?"

"Cool it, Clyde," said Lee Roy. "Hump and I figgered that the fewer people who knew, the less chance there'd be for a real feathers-on scandal. Why, we even told Delamain that ole Gus was on a Top Secret project and to tell ever'one that he was on leave. 'Top Secret' bein' the oney way to keep John's mouth shut."

Well, at least now we knew what Lee Roy did at LIT.

"And it had to be done," Hump repeated.

"Why, Hump?" I asked. "Why did it have to be done."

Hump looked startled. "Because he was using *my* machine, in *my* agency, to conduct *his* business. And I can't allow that."

"But jail, Hump? There's something wrong with the proportion."

"Lookee, LuLuBelle, what that mother did was a criminal act and criminals go to jail. Or they should do."

"What would you have done if you'd been me, Bea? Asked him politely to remove his files? We had to make an example of him."

"Sure, that's why you kept it hushed! How in hell can you make an example of something no one knows about?" Don yelled.

"I think Hump ast LuLuBelle here a question, Clyde. Whyn't you let her answer?"

"What would you have done, Bea?" asked Hump, quietly.

"I'd have wiped out his files. Erased them. And not said a word to anyone."

"Just an itty-bitty wrist slap, huh LuLuBelle?"

Don said, "You think wiping out the record of the investment portfolios of 100 clients is a wrist-slap? You dumb jerk, it would have torpedoed Gus's career as an investment manager; it might have got him sued by at least one of those guys; it would have kept his private stuff off the big computer forever; and he'd probably be around now when Carfil needs him. And if that's not enough, we'd have stayed out of the scandal we're probably going to get into.

"So why didn't you do that, Hump?"

Hump frowned. "We did wipe it. I suppose that might have been enough. I just didn't think it through. Well, it's too late to stop it now. "

"Just a red-hot minute, Clyde. Somewhere in your bleeding heart speech you left out that the guy's a criminal and criminals belong in the clink."

"Fuck off, jerk." Don grabbed my arm and hauled me out of the room.

As we got to the corridor, Don said, "You know, they do have a point."

"It would be a lot more convincing if they hadn't made the effing point while they were using *LIT's* equipment on the *Department's* time to play their dumb-assed game. And if you say 'Hump's o.k.', I'll brain you."

I stalked back to my office, kicked the door shut, and stared out the window. I didn't notice the Arts and Industry Building. The plane roaring overhead annoyed me.

And that completes the cast of characters. Who would have guessed that within a few months just about every member of that motley crew would be suspected of murder.

CHAPTER 6

February 13 (cont) - 14, 1990

I picked up my buzzing intercom. It was Don. "Let's get out of this joint and go someplace decent for lunch. We can take the Metro up to the high rent district."

To Don, 'someplace decent' is anything other than a stand-up hot dog from a sidewalk vendor. And anything tonier than McDonald's is reserved for celebrations, Secretary's Week, or as a cure for severe emotional trauma. His suggestion of a Metro ride to get lunch suggested the depth of the man's depression. We were on our way down the subway's steps before I broke in on his gloom. "Where are we going?"

"I forgot the name of the restaurant up there. You know."

"Don, the northwest quadrant of Washington probably has the highest density of restaurants in America outside of Manhattan. 'The restaurant up there' doesn't cut it as a description."

"You know, the cafeteria we went to last time."

Sholl's! The subway ride would cost more than lunch; Don was alive and well after all.

Sholl's Cafeteria, on K St., is an incredible institution. It was founded in 1928 by a man with a Christian vision of how the world should work, and he created a prototype of that world in his business. The outward symbols of the vision are the various religious pictures and exhortations which decorate the walls. "The family that prays together, stays together' is served up daily with the liver and onions. More importantly, the place seems to be run along the lines of a Christian commune. It is commonly believed -- and I have no cause to doubt it -- that everyone who works there is given an ownership interest in the enterprise. They certainly behave as if they have one.

Sholl's also demonstrates a singular interest in the well-being of its customers. The food is both good and cheap. Arguably, it has the best rhubarb pie in the world. It certainly has the best pecan rolls for breakfast.

But the truly unique essence of Sholl's is neither its food, nor its prices, nor its religiosity. It is the virtually tribal homogeneity of the people who work there. These people -- except for the fact that almost all of them are women -- are not similar in any accepted sense of the word. They are of every conceivable color and nationality and each wave of immigration brings with it another dollop for the Sholl's melting pot. Nonetheless, they all look alike and, perhaps even more remarkably, they sound alike. There is a Sholl's accent as there is a Harvard accent. It resembles the Hungarian speech patterns more than any other, but it is not quite that. I think they must have some sort of training school because every employee -- Hispanic, Black, Oriental, whatever -- has the same speech pattern. I have often dreamed of writing a Broadway musical about Sholl's. The servers, dressed in starched white and ladling up vegetable soup, would sing a chorus of "Muv along, muv along, next pliz, next pliz", while the customers high-kick atop the steam table.

So Sholl's it was.

We "muvved along" the line and, eventually spotting a free table, sat down with our pot roast and pie.

"I can't believe I was that wrong about the guy," Don said.

"Hump?"

"Yeah. He might be right about Gus. I dunno. There are a lot of things involved. But I'd never believe he would just shoot from the hip like that. Not talk it over with us. You don't just send a guy to jail without trying to find some other way to do it. I suppose Lee Roy talked him into it."

"Come on, Don. He chose to consult with Lee Roy instead of anyone else. And since he must know what a bastard Lee Roy is, he must have known the advice he was going to get. I think he wanted to stick it to Gus and he was just looking for someone to tell him it was the right thing to do."

"Yeah. Jesus, even talking to Delamain would have been better than Lee Roy. At least Delamain would have known you couldn't stop a scandal by pretending Gus was on vacation. How could I have been so wrong about that fat slob?"

We ate our pot roast and watched, enchanted, while a high-level-State-Department-type asked a low-level-Washington-bag-lady-type if he could share her table. She moved her considerable pile of belongings from a chair to the floor and graciously consented.

"How did an ass like Delamain ever get an SES slot?"

Don shrugged. "He used to be a pretty good technical man. He was at Defense when they decided to make Ada the standard computer language. John was in on the early Development of it; was one of the team that pushed it and then installed it at DoD. There was a helluva fight about it – the Services had damn near thirty years of installed base in other languages and they didn't want to convert. You couldn't blame them, really. Delamain led the fight from the Secretary's office and won it. I gotta admit, he did a good job. Aside from anything else, he probably knows Ada and what it can do better than anyone around except maybe Gus."

"So what happened to him?"

"He got promoted over his head. He doesn't know anything except programming languages. Export policy is way beyond him. He doesn't even know anything about the other technical areas. You might have noticed that he stays out of things like biotech. He turns all the technical discussions into software considerations and all his policy decisions hinge on what's good for his career."

We started on the rhubarb pie.

"How's the RIF panel going?"

"I was gonna talk to you about that. Ben's getting hit."

"Uh oh. Can you protect him?"

"Yeah, I think so. The guy that's gonna hit him doesn't look too bad, though. Do you wanna keep Ben? Hump would rather let him go."

"I'm beginning to think that Hump would like to pull the wings off everything that flies. Does he know Ben is on the hit list?"

"Naw. I wanted to talk to you first. Why do you want Ben? It doesn't look like he's ever going to finish that report."

"Doesn't matter. I'm sending the drafts over to the trade people as soon as they come out of Ginny Jean's machine. If it were anyone but Ben, they would be finished products. The only thing that's preventing them from being 'finals' is his obsession with format and the trade guys couldn't care less about that. They're using the drafts."

"Do they think they're any good?"

"Damn right. They're the basis of the American high-tech trade policy. And I don't think anyone else in the world, let alone in Government, would be as meticulous about the statistics. We can't afford to lose him just because Hump thinks he's a pain in the ass."

Don thought for a while. "It's not just us that would lose him. He'd be gone to the whole Government. He doesn't have anyplace to bump to."

"Could STAB pick him up?"

"They don't have any slots."

"Then you've got to protect him, Don. On top of the fact that we need him, he's the sole support of his mother. He needs the job."

"Ouch. His father dead?"

"Suicide. According to Ben, his Dad decided one day that life was too much trouble so he drove his clunker into the garage, ran a tube from the exhaust into the car, and sat there reading Marcuse until the monoxide got to him."

"You gotta be kidding? No one would do that unless there was some real reason."

"Maybe. But that's the story Ben told me. And Ben doesn't even think it's unreasonable. Ben does not look upon human life as sacred."

"Well, you're the one who has to live with him. Write a defense and I'll try to protect him. But don't tell Hump."

"My lips are sealed."

We finished our coffee.

The next day, after a morning of playing telephone-tag, I finally got through to Gordon Bryce at the Subcommittee.

"Have you had a chance to talk to anyone about LIT?"

"I just finished talking to the Chairman and he's interested," Bryce said. "But he's interested in a lot of other things, too. You'll need something really potent to grab him."

"I'm not sure we have anything far enough along to risk a high-profile demonstration. You don't think he'd go for a standard briefing?"

"Anything's possible; trade's a big thing with him. But LIT's not exactly the glamour agency of the Western World. You got a lot of competition for his attention. So you gotta give him a reason to bother about you."

"He's from Florida and we've got an important NASA project. But I don't know whether it'll be in demo condition in time to do the budget any good. I know we can put a helluva chalk-talk together and I'm pretty sure NASA will cooperate."

"Jesus. A demo would be better but I'll try."

"Do you think you can get Jaeklin, too? He's on Appropriations and we can get both committees at one shot."

"You don't want much. I'll see what I can do. The Authorization hearings are scheduled for late April. Try to shoot for then. And call me at the end of next week." Bryce hung up. What a crazy way to make a living! All the time I spent in graduate school and all the time that I spent at the Admin Studies Center and no one ever mentioned that most of our days were devoted to sheer nonsense.

I mused about this. Professor Graham Allison came close when he talked about how the government made decisions during the Cold War. He remarked that everyone thought the point of any Department's decision-making was to play the chess game so as to capture the Soviet's king. Not so, he said. The point of the State Department's decision making was to capture the Defense Department's king. Or something like that.

But I don't think even Graham Allison understood how truly loony we are.

I shook myself out of it and sat looking at the phone. Maybe we could bring it off. If I could find a line to the Senate.

CHAPTER 7

February 20, 1990

The phone was ringing as I approached my office. I sprinted the last few yards. "Beatrice Goode speaking."

"You sound breathless. Who's chasing you?"

"Fifteen budget analysts with axes. Who is this?"

Chuckles on the other end of the line. "The sixteenth. This is Freddy Langsteth. Gotcha."

"Whoops. Present company excluded, of course. What can I do for you?"

"I've got questions left over from the briefing. Thought you might prefer to discuss them before I send them over in writing."

"You bet. Do you want to talk about them over the phone or would you rather meet?"

"Meet, if we can find a congenial time. Feel as if my ear is growing a telephone cord. How's lunch?"

"Not great. I've got some visiting industry firemen due. Can it wait until dinner?"

"Hold on, I'll check." There was a short pause while Freddy inquired as to whether LIT was on the critical list. "Dinner's fine. What time and where?"

"Why don't we go over to The Smithsonian Residents Lounge about six?"

"Lady," Freddy said, "after a day at OMB, I need a drink at six."

"You can get one at the lounge. That belongs to the part of The Smithsonian that isn't Government."

"Sold then, see you at six. Bring your budget figures."

It was only after I hung up that I recalled that the good Ms. Langsteth was rumored to be gay. Please God, I can't cope with a pass.

As I walked past Stevie's door on my way to the staff meeting, he hailed me. "Hey, Bea, are you going to get a briefing on the export tech assessments?"

"Yeah. Delamain's going to give us one right now. Would you like to sit in?"

Steve's face lit up. "Do you think Hump would mind? I'd like to know more about the technical areas and I got a little time right now."

"C'mon."

Steve joined me. The little guy was a good executive officer. One of bureaucracy's inherent problems is that the administrative side of the house is usually divorced from the people who carry out the organization's missions. Because of this, the administrators seldom have the faintest clue as to what's important. And since the administrators are the ones who control the budget, there are often some really weird expenditures. Steve Chandler was one of the few execs who took an interest in the substantive work of his agency. He wasn't often fooled by the likes of Delamain.

John was shuffling his papers in the conference room when we seated ourselves. "Are we discussing the budget?" he asked Steve.

"No. I invited Steve to join us," I answered. "He has some influential friends in the Senate and I thought it would be helpful if he heard your briefing, John."

Steve opened his mouth and I kicked him on the ankle. He closed his mouth.

"Well, well," said John. "I didn't realize you had friends in powerful places. You should sit in on some more of these."

Don came in. "Hi. You staying, Steve? Good."

Don sat down and began to describe the intricacies of setting up the spring's softball schedule.

John interrupted with the fascinating story of the day he played first base against a team that included the third cousin of the wife of the Speaker of the House. As he was describing the first foul ball I tore a sheet off my yellow pad and scrawled, "Do you think Alex can come up with a demo by mid-April? That's nearly two months." I passed the note to Don.

He read it, wrote, and passed it back. "He can probably have something. No big production and no earlier. Talk to him before we surface it here."

I was giving Don a thumbs-up when Hump walked in.

"Sorry I'm late. Damn dog." Hump aimed some coffee toward his cup.

"Hump, why don't you take the dog's collar in a notch?"

Hump glowered at me. "It's as tight as it will go. It's just too big for her. O.K., John, what's the news from export?"

"Isn't Lee Roy coming?"

"He's going to a meeting for me at GSA. He can give this one a miss."

Don grunted. "He can give 'em all a miss."

"You still sore-assed?" Hump laughed. "You don't enjoy making that kind of decision, Don. Leave them to Lee Roy. It makes him feel important."

"What?" Delamain asked. "What decisions?"

"Nothing much, John. Let's get on with the briefing."

John riffled his papers, cleared his throat, and pronounced, "We investigated the possibility of three export items this month. They are, first, a man-made germ that the pharmaceutical house claims has great potential in fighting the common cold. Second, there is a guidance system for bicycles. Third, is an artificial intelligence-based telephone answering system which will screen and answer incoming calls. We spent five man months on the three investigations and I am happy to say that complete reports will be ready for the high-tech export committee next week." John looked around the table. I wondered if he was waiting for applause.

"What was the verdict, John?" Don asked.

"Mixed reviews. The problem with the biotech thing is more an ethical one than anything else. I'm not sure that's our business, but the gal who vetted it -- Carrie Barnar -- thinks we ought to bring it up."

I poured myself a cup of coffee. "What's the issue, John?"

"Well, the bug isn't being made for sale in this country -- it's still going through the FDA testing process. The Europeans aren't as rigorous as we are and the tests have satisfied their requirements. We can manufacture and sell it there. But Carrie doesn't think we should export until we're sure it's safe."

"LIT doesn't make policy," Hump pointed out. "We just report on market and security."

"There's no question on those two points," Delamain said. "God knows there's a market for a cure for the common cold. And there doesn't seem to be any use for that germ in chemical warfare."

"Still," Don said, "she's got a point."

"Yeah. But not in the LIT report. I'll bring it up when the Export Committee meets. What's with the bicycle?"

John laughed. "This is a crock. It's a bicycle with a sensor mounted on the front. When the bike approaches a solid object, the sensor automatically causes the bike to veer. There isn't anything new in the technology -- no security grounds for denying export permission, but we can't see any reason for the Government to help..." he looked at his notes, "the PedalSafe Corporation."

The door opened and Lee Roy slouched in. "D'I miss anythin'?"

Hump shook his head. "GSA meeting finish early?"

"For all I know, it's still goin' on and will be goin' on 'til the middle of next week. Those guys are boring. I stayed for ever'thin' that matters to us and left."

"And what mattered to us?" I asked.

"Nuthin'. That's why I'm here now."

"Finish with PedalSafe, John," Hump said.

"Well, that's about all for them. We didn't see much of a market anywhere, although PedalSafe thinks there is a lot of potential in the Third World. I mean, who wants a bicycle that won't go where you point it? It could veer away from a wall and into something a lot worse."

Lee Roy cackled. "It wouldn't be the first time them niggers landed themselves in a pile of shit."

"What's the last one?"

"Now, that one is very interesting. Very interesting indeed. It's an automated answering machine that parses incoming calls and either forwards them, takes a message, or rejects them. It will also prioritize the messages it takes. It looks promising. Very promising."

I was intrigued. "How does it work?"

"On the same principle as expert systems. You program instructions; tell the machine who you want to talk to, what subjects you want to talk about, who and what's most important. There's a voice output on the system and when someone calls, the machine asks who it is and what it's about and then it follows the instructions. It makes real use of artificial intelligence in that it learns, over time. That is, if it knows how you've dealt with similar, previous messages, it will handle them the same way after that. Very very impressive."

"I dunno," Hump said. "You know the problem with telecommunications devices. The Europeans and the Japs don't like to let foreign technology in. I'm not sure the market is big enough for the Government to get involved."

"That's the beauty of it, Hump."

Delamain was clearly pushing the product. "We're not going to make it here. ZapaCall is working out licensing agreements overseas. The device will be made in the country of sale. It's still a problem, but a lot smaller one than a straight export."

Hump shook his head. "Can't recommend it, John. Security problem."

"Did we miss something?"

"Yeah. That software is awfully close to something the Defense Department is using. Who did the investigation?"

"Chin and Bertolli."

"Send them up to see me this afternoon. We'd better rewrite that one."

"Sure thing, Hump, we wouldn't want to miss one, would we?"

"But Hump," Steve said, "why should we bar an export just because DoD uses the technology? They use lotsa technologies -- like telephones -- and we don't stop exporting them."

Hump looked at Steve as if he were noticing him for the first time. "Can't explain it, kid. Classified."

Steve subsided.

"How you doing on the Hill, Bea?"

"Progressing. I think we might be able to get the House Authorization Committee over here in mid-April for a briefing on Tarzan. I'll talk to Alex so we can get the planning started."

John lit up. "Not a briefing, Bea. Think big. A real demonstration that'll lay 'em in the aisles."

Lee Roy chimed in. "Dancin' girls."

I looked at Don. He looked at me. Mutual panic.

"Not April," Hump said. "I'll be on annual leave. Mauve wants to go to Holland for the tulips this year."

"If we schedule after April it'll be too late to help with Authorization's mark-up. And besides, I'm not sure...."

Hump smiled. "Not later, earlier. March."

"But Hump," Don yelped, "Alex won't have anything."

"Sure he will," Delamain said. "It might not be the best package, but I think the Congressmen will enjoy seeing work in progress. They must get tired of all the slick pitches they see."

"Why don't we call Alex in and ask him?" I said.

Lee Roy tsked at me. "LuLuBelle, if you ast the troops anythin' they say 'no way'. That way you'll be real grateful when they come up with somethin'. Naw. You gotta tell 'em, not ast 'em."

Hump nodded. John, who was watching Hump, nodded vigorously. "What we should do is get a mockup of a space vehicle, see, and have the demonstration inside the mockup." He thought for a minute. "Unless we can get a real vehicle. Can we get a vehicle Hump?"

"Maybe. But then we'd have to have the demo at one of the NASA sites."

"Right. And that would look like a NASA demo instead of ours. We can put the mockup on the roof. That should add a little, uh, verisimilitude."

"...to an otherwise bald and unbelievable narrative," I finished. "March is too soon. Even April may be too soon for anything credible." I shut my mouth before I said anything else. It would be bad form to call my superiors a bunch of idiots.

"Don't be so negative, Bea," Hump said. "Carfil can get something together. It doesn't have to be anything new -- just so it's flashy. The Congressmen can't tell the difference."

"I dunno," Don put in. "I don't know the backgrounds of the Members, but I think some of the staffers are sharp."

"What do we do if the weather's lousy?" Steve asked.

"Move it into the auditorium. Set it up for March, Bea. Early in the month -- later I'm going to be busy getting ready for the trip to Holland. O.K., if that's all, we can adjourn." Hump got up and moved toward the door, John and Lee Roy trailing.

"Hey, did you hear about the Yid and the Guinea..."

I picked up my pen and paper and turned to Don. "I think I blew it. Tulips!"

Ben stuck his head in the door. "I couldn't help overhearing. I always knew Puce was a blooming idiot."

"That's Mauve, Ben. Not Puce. Mauve." Ben grinned as Steve hurried past him.

Don, Ben, and I walked into the reception area. Frances Monk was hovering over Lenore's desk. Lenore was nowhere in sight. Frances nodded to us and scurried across the reception room and into her office. We heard her safe being opened.

Ben looked at the phone messages on the desk. "Oh, oh. The OPM auditor is asking for a meeting with Hump." He flipped through Hump's appointment calendar. "Doesn't look too promising until mid-March. Hump is going to a Tech Society meeting in London next week. Frances should be safe for another month."

Don looked exasperated. "Get out of there before Lenore catches you."

"Just curious," Ben said. He trotted off.

Don walked back down the hall with me. We heard Steve yelling at his broker as we moved past his office. Don waited while I called the Committee staff room. Bryce had no problem with the change in date -- the Committee was less frantic in March than in April. "Just remember that the Members have a short attention span. If it comes off more than a month before the Hearings it better be pretty damn spectacular or they'll forget about you."

"Not likely that a briefing will do it, if that's what you mean."

We set it up for March 9, which was as late as I thought I could get away with.

"Rats," I said.

"Shit," Don said.

"You got any good news, Don?"

"Yeah. As a matter of fact, I do. Ben's safe for this round. Good defense. Well, you better tell Alex." He left.

I made my way downstairs, rather hoping that Alex wouldn't be there. I didn't want to tell him. My luck, however, continued rotten. I could hear him, in full voice, from the staircase. I reached his office just as he hit the chorus of 'Prithee, Pretty Maiden...'

"Don't ask," I said.

Alex rounded on me. "Why didn't you tell me you were a widow?"

"The occasion didn't arise. Who did tell you?"

"Don."

"Indeed? And what was the occasion? Did he just bump into you in the hall and say, 'In case you were wondering, old chap...'"

"No. He was preparing a sandwich board on the subject. What the hell's the matter with you? Why shouldn't he tell me?"

I sat down. "I'm sorry, Alex. No reason in the world. I've had a lousy morning and I'm about to ruin yours."

Alex looked at me warily.

"Our Authorization Committee is arriving on March 9 and you're on the agenda with a demonstration of Tarzan."

Alex no longer looked wary; he looked thunderstruck.

"You guys are out of your goddam minds! Look at this lab; does it look like I can get a demo together by March? Tell 'em they'll get a briefing."

"Alex, don't kill the messenger. Get together with Delamain and try to come up with something credible. The U.S. Congress will be here for a demonstration on March 9."

Alex glared at me. "Then you'd better let me get to work." He turned back to his bench and I left. There was no singing in the halls.

I called Hope Lahti when I got back to my office. "Was Gordon Bryce helpful?"

I filled Hope in on LIT's Hill progress and Gordon's lack of same.

"That's fine. I'll talk to Gordon and remind him that Jaeklin is important."

"I don't understand the committee structure, Hope. I thought that if a Member was on Appropriations he couldn't also be on another committee."

"That's usually true. The Leadership has to make an exception. And they made one for Jaeklin."

"Is he that important?"

"He's being groomed as a possible Presidential. Wank is retiring in '92 and Jaeklin will run for the Senate seat. If he makes it, they'll move him onto the national stage."

I thought of the cables strewn about Alex's lab and felt sick.

"Speaking of the Senate, Hope, do you know anyone there who might do us some good?"

There was a short silence. "I'll see. I'll call you back."

Hope hung up.

I spent the afternoon showing the visiting industrialists around LIT and explaining to them why it would be inappropriate for the Federal Government to subsidize all of their overseas marketing expenses. I think I made a hash of it.

Freddy was waiting when I got to the Residents Lounge at six. We brought our macaronis to a table and proceeded to talk budget through dinner. Freddy seemed to be searching for a way to ensure that, if she recommended a budget cut, it wouldn't result in our RIFFing someone good. She seemed to be pushing for the axe to fall on Delamain. I had caught on to the Washington Monument game, however, and kept offering up Alex. Freddy looked at me sourly, "Cut the crap," she said.

I laughed. "Look, I don't like Delamain any more than you do. And if the truth be known, I can think of half a dozen other little LITTies that we could do without very nicely, thank you. But like John, they are senior. And you've been a Fed long enough to know that they'll bump our best and brightest. Unless you know something I don't know."

Freddy grimaced. "You got me. Situation is that you're going to lose the appeal."

"But Freddy..."

"Hear me out. I'm going to recommend full funding. Going to be overruled because we have to come up with the cuts. Get your ass over to the Hill. If you can get Authorization to restore, I can promise you that we'll support it privately in Appropriations. Won't notice your Hill activities. That's the best I can do. Good luck."

I nodded. "O.K."

"I'm going to get that drink now."

The waiter responded to her signal and Freddy asked him for a Scotch.

"No got skutch," he said.

"Sure you do," I said. "Go look."

He ambled off.

"This is a lonely town for a single woman," Freddy remarked.

"It is." I wondered if the pass was about to come.

"Worst thing about a divorce is that it leaves you feeling so worthless. Even when you're the one who leaves. Still feel rejected. If there's anything good to say about widowhood, it's that at least you don't feel deliberately abandoned."

"Don't you believe it. I was literally and irrationally angry at Harry when he was killed. I stayed mad for a year."

The waiter came back. "No got skutch."

Freddy reached into her briefcase and drew out a pencil and pad. She wrote, in big print, 'S-C-O-T-C-H' and drew facsimiles of some common brand labels beneath. The waiter looked at her handiwork. The light of comprehension washed over his features.

"Aha! Not skutch. Skawtch." He marched off.

Freddy nodded. "The real problem," she said, "is getting laid. Where the hell does a 55 year old divorcee go to get laid in this town?"

So much for the veracity of the rumor mill.

"Freddy, I don't even know where a 35 year old widow goes to get laid in this town."

The waiter came back, triumphantly bearing a water glass filled to the brim with amber liquid. He plunked it down before Freddy. She tasted it, gingerly. "Scotch," she pronounced.

She looked at the waiter. "May I have a doggy bottle?"

I drove out of the lot and pointed the car toward the bridge. "Husband-of-mine, where does a 35 year old widow go to get laid?"

After today, there was scant chance that the adorable Carfil would speak to the messenger from the Director's office, let alone lay her.

CHAPTER 8

March 2 - 7, 1990

Alex's vigorous off-key tenor wafted through the corridor. 'Faint heart never won Fair Lady...' Things must be going well in the lab. I suppressed an urge to belt out the 'Hallelujia Chorus' and knocked on his door.

Alex broke off in the middle of a particularly sonorous 'lady'. "C'min."

This was our first encounter since I had broken the news of the Committee visit. I wasn't at all sure of the reception I was going to get, but a progress report from Alex was needed before the demo could be set up.

I needn't have worried. "Have a lemon square."

I chomped on a cookie. "Dr. Carfil, I simply must have that recipe."

Alex grinned. "I'll make a lab assistant out of you yet."

"How's it going, Alex? Are we going to have a demonstration?"

"You betcha." He stopped grinning. "Delamain is making a circus out of it. Talk to him, will you. He's put so many bells and whistles on the demo that nobody's going to notice Tarzan."

"I have talked to him and a fat lot of good it did. The man is obsessed with that stupid mockup. He's got everything choreographed right down to the final shuffle-off-to-Buffalo. It wouldn't surprise me if he chalked our places on the floor of the roof. Unfortunately, the ass not only outranks me, he outranks Don."

"Won't Stafford do something?"

"At the moment, Hump has taken himself off to London. Besides, he liked the idea of a space-ship mockup."

Alex made a face. "Listen, Bea, I want to apologize for the other day."

I tried to think of what Alex might be apologizing for. "What did you do that I don't know about?"

He looked sheepish. "Pitched you out of my lab. Steve told me you and Don argued against nailing me to a March date. Thanks."

"We aren't such hot arguers." I took another cookie. "Tell me what Tarzan is going to do so I can help plan the circus."

Alex spent the next half-hour describing the capabilities of his machine. Essentially, the thing would perform two relatively simple tasks and one complex blockbuster. Nowhere near the complexity of the tasks it would perform in space, but impressive enough for the early going.

Tarzan had a brain -- of a sort. Physically, the brain was located on a disk within the computer. Like the brain of a newborn baby, at first Tarzan's brain had no real memory, not having anything to remember. Tarzan did have a computer's equivalent of a nervous system and some "instinctive" reactions. A baby's instinct tells it to breathe. A computer's instinct tells it to boot (that is, to prepare to remember things and follow instructions). As a baby grows up, it acquires a real memory through experience. Tarzan acquired his memory when Alex wrote a program and engraved it on Tarzan's brain.

For the demonstration, Alex would sit at a microcomputer, push the "boot" button and type in the magic words that would cause Tarzan to remember what he was there for and to start following instructions. Those instructions would be transmitted through cables that attached the arms to the micro. When the instructions reached the arms, they would go into motion. Alex had programmed several tasks. The arms would open a jar. They would pick up a stool and bring it over for Delamain to sit on (Guess whose idea?) Then, most impressive, Delamain would push a toy dump truck across the floor; one of the arms would grab and hold it; the other arm would pick up a screw driver and take the wheels off. And that was a tour de force.

"Will it really work, Alex?"

"Oh, you Bear of little faith. Of course it works. Delamain and I have been testing it all week."

I had a vision of John Delamain on his hands and knees pushing a dump truck across the floor of the roof -- over and over and over.

"Too bad you couldn't find some use for his rubber duckie. Congratulations, Alex."

"Uh, Bea, would you like to come out for a slightly premature celebration tonight? The D.C. Buttercups are doing 'Patience' and I've got two tickets."

And there it was. With all my thinking about Alex, how come I hadn't decided what I'd do if he asked me out? I hadn't gone out with a man since Harry died. It was still too soon. I wasn't ready. I opened my mouth to say no, politely and regretfully. I said, "I'd love to."

"If you don't mind leaving from here, we could have dinner first."

I nodded.

"Is six o.k.?"

I nodded again, grabbed a cookie, and fled.

Delamain in person intercepted me on my way back to the office. "Bea, about Hump's speech."

"I'm writing it, John. I'm writing it."

"Well, that's just it. He doesn't read very well. You know, he doesn't project. I think maybe he shouldn't have the speech written out."

"John, I am aware that Hump delivers all speeches to his belly. He probably has the best educated navel in Washington. But everything else we've tried is worse."

"I think we should just give him an outline. Maybe with a few key phrases written out on 3x5 cards. If we rehearse him a few times that should go much better than him chanting a speech."

"It should. Are you willing to guarantee that he'll be here to rehearse?"

John frowned. "Well, he certainly knows how important this demonstration is. My God, Carfil and I have been slaving for days..."

"I know. Playing with your toys on the roof. Are you willing to guarantee that Hump will rehearse?"

"Now look, Bea, I don't like to pull rank," like hell he didn't, "but when Hump's not here, I'm in charge and I'm telling you to give him 3x5s. And I want to see them by close of business Monday. That will give me time to make changes before Hump gets back on Wednesday."

"Amen," I said and made my way back to my office. I briefly considered writing the outline for John's delectation and a back-up speech for Hump when he saw the outline and had a conniption. I decided against the speech on the grounds that if Hump had stayed where he belonged, he wouldn't have to face the Committee naked and afraid.

I finished the outline about 2:00 and, lunchless, headed for the Department of Labor and the maiden meeting of the Interagency Committee on Technology and Employment.

As it happens, it was an interesting meeting. About half of the economists there were turning themselves and their statistics inside out in order to prove that the adoption of labor-saving technologies would result in more jobs. The other half of the economists were performing similar contortions in order to prove that the adoption of labor-saving technologies would result in some job loss, but it would be worse if we went our labor-intensive way because the rest of the world would undersell us. Another two or three neo-Great Society economists were erudite Luddites.

I was sitting next to a very tall, very skinny man with a Western accent. His badge informed me that he was Doc Flammihand of the Bureau of Mines. He kept up a steady counterpoint of homespun anecdotes throughout the presentations. We broke for coffee at 3:30 and Doc and I wandered over to the coffeepot together.

"You been at LIT long?"

I laughed. "No one's been at LIT long. We're only a year old."

"Wal, now, I reckon that's right. I understand you stole the best budget analyst out of our region."

"I don't think so. LIT doesn't carry a budget analyst of its own. The exec. officer covers."

"I don't mean *you* stole her. I mean OMB stole her for you."

"Ah. Langsteth. That's right, she did come from BoM. It's encouraging to know that she's well thought of. We need all the help we can get right now."

"Wal, that's right. But isn't it a little sticky with Hump Stafford there and all?"

I set my coffee cup down carefully. "Why should it be sticky?"

"Wal, I'm not one to gossip, you know, but it sure is bound to come out and you might as well get it straight."

"Doc," I said, "give."

And give he did. The events had occurred more than five years ago when Hump, married to his first wife, was running a DoD lab in Silicon Valley. Freddy, also married, was at a nearby BoM installation. Hump had been drinking heavily and, his friends believed, undergoing severe depression. "He was a handsome fella then, Miz Goode, a handsome fella. I could hardly credit it when I saw all the weight he put on up here."

In brief, Freddy took that handsome fella to her bosom, nursed him to health, and sent him -- renewed -- back to his lab. By that time, both marriages were in shambles.

Shortly thereafter, Hump met Mauve. Small wonder that he spent the OMB briefing trying to dodge Freddy.

The chairman called us back to hear the last of the economists.

Don was waiting for the elevator when I got back to the LIT building. "Where ya been?"

"At the Technology and Employment meeting."

"Anything interesting?"

I wondered momentarily whether I should tell Don about Hump's escapade with Freddy and decided against it. Don was disillusioned enough with the fat man. "Just a bunch of economists placed end to end and pointing in every direction."

We got on the elevator. "I'm sitting in for Hump at the Export Control meeting on Monday. You got time to come with me? The Departmental brass should start knowing who you are. I don't want them hearing your name for the first time from someone on the Hill."

"I'll make the time. I thought Delamain was panting to take Export Control."

"Hump told me to go and just stick with all the LIT positions. I don't like it."

We got off the elevator. "What's wrong?"

"I'm not sure. Remember that telephone answering device that Zapacall wants to export?"

I nodded. "The thing with the security problem."

"Yeah. I read the rewrite of the analysis and it doesn't say much except that it's a lot like a technology DoD is using. I went down to Chin's office and asked him if Hump had explained and Chin said no. Just to change it. Chin didn't understand why but Hump said it had a high classification and he couldn't explain."

"And?"

"I'm cleared for everything Hump's cleared for and I don't know anything that should stop export. I can't support our document."

"What are you going to do about it?"

"See if I can get it tabled until Hump gets back, I guess. Let's see how it plays when we get there."

We walked to our respective offices. As I was entering mine, Ben and Steve came around the corner on their way to the elevator. Ben's ears were on alert.

Alex walked into my office at six. "Where do you want to eat?"

"What are the choices?"

"Chaumiere's if you want French. Chinese. Japanese, if you like raw fish. Or we can get some really terrible chili in Alexandria."

"Do I detect a man who wants some really terrible chili?"

"Yeah."

We ransomed Alex's car and headed for Alexandria. The chili was appropriately terrible. The production of 'Patience' was more terrible yet. I loved every minute of it.

After the performance, Alex said "Uh, Bea, would you like to come over to my house and make some cookies?"

I gaped at him. "Did you just ask me to come to your house to make cookies?"

"Well, that or anything else you want to do."

I was still giggling when we pulled up to Alex's townhouse in Old Town. It was a cute little neo-Federalist house, three stories high. A soft, golden light shone through the ground floor windows, their protective grillwork making shadows on the pavement. Alex unlocked the dead bolt and we went in. My giggles deserted me and I stood in the middle of his living room wondering what on earth I was going to do now that I was there. I think if I'd had my car I would have cut and run.

Alex took my coat. He went into the kitchen and put the coffee on. I wandered around the living room looking at his possessions. Alex came out of the kitchen, put his arms around me and we kissed. Well, I thought, I guess I know what I'm going to do.

Alex went back into the kitchen and turned off the coffee pot. He kissed me again. "Will we make love?"

"Yes. But gently, Alex. It's been a very long time."

I hadn't anticipated that making love after those years of abstinence would be so -- different. It was almost like a book that you reread after a decade; as each scene begins you remember how it went, but damned if you can remember what happens in the next scene. Alex was gentle and Alex was very good at what he was doing. Sensations that I had nearly forgotten were recalled and then happened. And my God, nothing could ever be better.

I woke up the next morning feeling more than a little sore and altogether marvelous. I reached out for Alex and found myself groping in empty space. Panic.

Then the smell of coffee and pancakes. I got out of bed and rooted around in Alex's closet until I found a moth-eaten old flannel robe. Chastely garbed, I made my entrance into the kitchen.

Alex was pouring batter into a pan and softly humming 'When All Night Long'. He turned as I padded in, set the bowl down and nuzzled me. We stood a moment, his arms around me, hands caressing the small of my back. "It's o.k., isn't it?"

"Very o.k."

Alex grinned. "Hey, preedy lady, you wan' anodder quick one?"

"Alla time, fella. But I want some pancakes more."

"Oh, my God!" Alex rushed back to his griddle and rescued his flapjacks in the nick of time.

We spent most of the morning gorging on pancakes and maple syrup. "Bea?"

"Mmph?"

"Is it really o.k.? Do you feel...uh..."

"What, Alex?"

"I dunno. Disloyal, maybe."

"Disloyal? You mean to Harry?"

"Was that his name? Your husband."

"Harry. He's dead, Alex. I've never believed in shrines. And even if I did, my body certainly isn't a suitable one."

"Hot dog!" said Alex.

We had anodder quick one.

Then we made cookies. Honest. Almond wafers.

Late in the afternoon, Alex ferried me to my garage.

I turned on the car radio and the first exultant notes of Mendelssohn's Italian Symphony burst forth. Those guys at the studio are psychic.

"*Harry*", I said, "*you wouldn't believe what happened last night. Harry? Harry?*"

Harry wasn't there. I patted the empty seat and grinned. "Wish me luck, boy-o."

I spent the rest of the weekend pottering around the house and thinking of almond wafers and Alex. There was no more sorting out of feelings. I knew how I felt. I loved Alex and I loved him on all levels. Sexual. Intellectual. Emotional. No complications. What I didn't know was what I was going to do about it. A pleasant roll in the hay with an attractive man is one thing. A casual affair with someone you love is something else again -- something intolerable, I think. Damn! If only I knew how Alex felt. Not something I could just ask him at intermission. Dear God, after one date. I found myself snickering at the thought. It was one helluva date.

Don and I arrived at the door of the Export Control meeting room simultaneously with a slim man in a blue blazer and a Western tan. He scrutinized Don's LIT badge and said, "Where's Hump?"

"Couldn't make it. I'm Don Cromarty and this is Bea Goode."

"George Grot, from DoTel. You been briefed?"

Don looked surprised. "Sure."

Grot smiled. "Fine. Fine." He patted Don on the arm and we entered the room.

The Deputy Secretary, a tubby gray-haired man, was already seated at the head of the table. He looked quizically at Don.

"I'm sitting in for Mr. Stafford, sir. This is my assistant, Dr. Goode. Bea, this is Deputy Secretary Gray."

The Deputy Secretary laughed. "I suppose it does take two of you to fill in for Hump. I'll miss him, though. He's the only guy around who's fatter than I am." He patted his tummy complacently. Then to the multitude, "Let's pass around the attendance sheet and get started. The first agenda item is, uh, Young!Young!Young!"

A voice from the far end of the table. "What's that?"

Gray looked as his notes. "Mink oil. Line of products that make you look young, young, young. Can't imagine any security problems. Let's hear from Gary first..."

Don leaned over and whispered in my ear. "Trade specialist. He'll describe the size of the export market and the competition."

"...then Dennis."

Don again. "FDA representative. He'll talk about efficacy and safety."

"You giving the industry's position, Lily?"

"With enthusiasm." From a beautifully groomed woman in a rose silk pantsuit.

The trade specialist cleared his throat and began popping statistics. Cosmetic exports on the rise since 1986. Imports also rising.

Don slid the attendance sheet to me and I studied it, matching names to faces. Lots of industry people. Big man sitting to the right of Gray was representing Lumber. Lily from cosmetics was next to him. Then Gary, trade specialist for the Cosmetics sector. Who was that guy in the clerical collar? I counted seats and positions on the attendance sheet. David Fortune, industry rep for banking services. Ask Don about that one. To Fortune's right, George Grot, industry rep for telecommunications peripherals. I slid the sheet to my right and focused on the presentations.

Young!Young!Young! occupied our attention (more or less) for about an hour. Decision: DoTI would put out an all-points to the consulates requesting that the product be mentioned in all speeches and press interviews, would press the case for easing import restrictions in Asia and the Soviet bloc, but would stay out of it in Western Europe. Lily assumed a half-a-loaf expression, excused herself with promises of next time, and departed.

"ZapaCall's next. Let's take that one then we can take a break. Fitz for trade. Don Cromarty's sitting in for Hump -- he'll take security -- who's industry?"

George Grot raised his hand. Fitz provided the statistics. On one side, it looked good: burgeoning market segment, no serious competitors, apparent high demand. On the other side, problems. The market segment was surrounded by non-tariff trade barriers. If ZapaCall was going to penetrate the international market, DoTI would have to mobilize behind it.

"Don?"

"I got a problem here. There may be a security issue but we need a little more time to study it. Move that we table until the next meeting."

"What?" From Grot. "Listen, guy, God knows I want to see a boost for the industry, but we can't fool around with national security. If there's a problem..."

"Hold it. I'm not saying we oughtta ship the thing to Russia tomorrow, for Godssake, I just want to table the decision until we have all our ducks in a row."

"How goddam much time..."

Gray let out a whistle and all heads swiveled. "Take a vote on tabling ." Vote passed with only Grot's dissent.

"OK", said Gray, "let's take a break and then catch the common cold before lunch."

Grot caught up with us at the coffee urn. He grabbed Don's arm. "I thought you said Hump briefed you."

"The technical guys briefed me. They need more time to look at it."

"That fat jerk! Some briefing." He retrieved his briefcase and stalked out of the room.

We chatted a bit with a few somewhat more amiable types until Gray whistled us back to our stations.

The FDA put an effective ki-bosh on the cure for the common cold. Good. Don didn't have to decide whether to bring up the ethical issues.

Don and I ate lunch in an obscure corner of the cafeteria. "What the hell do you think Grot was all about?"

I swallowed a mouthful of hard-boiled egg. "I can guess at a few things and I don't like any of them. You'd better get an explanation from Hump when he gets back from London. You're the only one with the same security clearances he's got and you have a demonstrated need to know. He can't stonewall you."

Don nodded and we finished lunch in uncharacteristic silence. The afternoon session on PedalSafe was uneventful, if unrewarding for the company.

Tuesday at the office defined chaos. Arrangements for the Congressional visit. Good news: Congressman Jaeklin would come. Bad news: No response from the Senate side. Good news: The Secretary of DoTI would come. Bad news: So would the NASA Administrator. Everyone would be joining us for lunch. No one would be there for lunch. From the Secretary's office: Could we possibly make room for some distinguished MIT academics led by the particularly Distinguished Professor Philip Lee? Yes, of course, Sir. From the Secretary's office: Never mind, the MIT people can't fit it into their schedule. Maybe a briefing next week. Hump hasn't called in. He's not at the hotel indicated on his itinerary. Who covers if he doesn't get back? Worse, what if he gets back too late to rehearse? Should we have invited

OMB? Too late to worry about it now. The space vehicle mockup won't be ready on time. Yes it will, sorry if we worried you. Regularly scheduled prayer sessions: please God, let the weather hold through Friday. And sandwiched in between, rehearsals on the roof.

Bless those rehearsals. Reality, sanity, in the midst of manufactured madness. Tarzan was really swinging. Again and again and again those arms reached out and unscrewed the cap, picked up the stool, and dismantled the dump truck. The programmed brain in the microcomputer issued the instructions and the arms moved. Surely, certainly, unvaryingly.

Hump appeared around 11:00 Wednesday morning and we all gathered for the obligatory staff meeting. I filled Hump in on who would -- and wouldn't -- be coming to the party. Delamain lovingly went over Tarzan's performance. The room was awash with a feeling of bonhomie and goodwill. And then Hump said, "Where's my speech, Bea?"

"I think I'd better let John tell you about it."

Hump looked puzzled. "John?"

"Well, Hump, I thought that it would be better if you had an outline, rather than a speech. It will give you some elbow room to adjust to your audience. So I directed Bea to do an outline for you and some 3x5s with key phrases. You really are very, very good when you extemporize and -- don't misunderstand me, Bea is a very accomplished speech writer, very accomplished, indeed -- but those fully written speeches do put you in a strait jacket and..."

John trailed off as Hump's face began shading from pink to red to purple. "You directed Bea to do what?"

"Well, Hump, if you and I sat down together, you could go over the speech a few times and, uh, gradually slip into something comfortable. I've cleared my decks so I have all of today and tomor..."

John stopped in midsentence. That was twice within five minutes; more likely that the earth would pause in orbit.

Lenore was standing at the conference room door. "Mr. Grot from DoTel is on the telephone. He says he has to speak with you urgently."

Hump picked up the conference room phone. "Hump Stafford, here. Yes, George. What? They did what? He did what?" Hump's face reversed its colorful progress. From purple to red to pink and finally to white. "Nothing that can't be fixed, George. I'll catch a plane and meet you in Denver tonight." He set the phone down gently and turned to Don. "Just what the hell kind of a game were you playing with the Export Control Committee?"

Don held his ground. "I couldn't explain our position on ZapaCall, so I asked them to table until you got back."

Hump turned from Don to John and back to Don again. I had never seen Hump angry before and it was awesome. His huge gobs of flesh were quivering. His teeth were literally chattering. He finally bellowed, "For chrisfuckinsake do I have to do everything myself? Lenore! Lenore! Get me on the next plane to Denver."

"But Hump," from Delamain. "Your speech rehearsal."

"Maybe you should get on the plane with him, Clyde. Your decks are cleared."

"Fuck the fuckinspeech."

Lenore materialized. "If you're going to get to Denver before midnight, you'll have to leave now, Mr. Stafford."

Hump paused only for a final glare at Don and John and tore out the door. A charging rhinoceros on his way to the airport.

Lenore called after him. "United, Mr. Stafford. From National, not Dulles." And to us. "Don't worry, I've booked him to be back before lunch on Friday. Some of us do think of those things." She sailed out.

"Jeez, Bea," Stevie said, "What're we gonna do about the speech?"

"Don't worry about it," Don answered.

"How can I not worry?" Stevie's voice rose to a strangled squeak.

I patted his shoulder. "Either Tarzan will sell himself or he won't and nothing Hump says will make any difference at all."

I nodded to John and returned to my office.

The only thing missing now was Murder.

THE LINKER

a computer program which links separately

written parts of a program together

CHAPTER 9

March 9, 1990

The day of the demo was clear, cold, and windy. Not a great day for a presentation on the roof, but tolerable. We were all in early. When I reached my office at 7:00, Ben was already there. Not doing anything, just pacing. Stevie arrived on the next elevator. Don fifteen minutes later. Then Delamain.

"Is the mockup here yet? Where's the mockup?"

I looked at Ben. "I went up to the roof at 6:30. It wasn't there then."

"What will we do?" Delamain was wringing his hands. I'd never seen anyone do that before.

"Well, we could panic," Don said. "But first let's go up to the roof and see if it got here between 6:30 and now."

"Why don't you guys go up," I suggested, "and I'll see if Alex is here yet. He might know something."

"I've been to the roof," said Ben. "I'll go with you, Bea."

What with one thing and another, I hadn't seen Alex alone since Saturday. I briefly considered braining Ben with the visitor's chair. "O.K., Ben, let's go."

We pointed Don, Stevie, and John skyward and walked down toward Alex's lab. 'I Have a Song to Sing-O' gave early indication of his presence. Ben and I arrived at the lab door.

"What is that song you sing?" The two of us in unison.

Alex threw back his head and carolled "Tee dee bump, tee dee bump, tee dee bump, tee dee bump. Good morning."

"I think so. Has the mockup arrived?"

"I don't know. I just got in. Let's go up and see."

Ben turned and led the way through the corridor. Alex followed me for a few steps and caught up. "I've just completed my evaluation," he whispered. You have a B+ fanny. With sufficient care, we might be able to bring it up to an A." There was a laying on of hand. "With diligence, hard work, some luck..."

Ben waited at the staircase. There was a laying off of hand. We walked up to the roof where the three men were standing, shivering. No mockup. The computer was there. The cables. Tarzan. But no mockup. The far side of the roof was empty.

"Well," offered Ben, "we can always say that it's a Space demonstration."

Don laughed and John pouted.

"It's only 8 o'clock," I said. "If it's not here by 9:30, let's meet in Hump's conference room and panic."

"Jeez, Hump!" Stevie swiveled around as if he expected Hump to materialize from the air vent. "Where's Hump? What'll we do?"

"We'll toss to see who gives the welcome speech," Don said. "We've all had as much rehearsal as Hump's had."

Alex was humming happily and poking his computer.

"Maybe Alex and I should run through it once more," John said. "We don't want anything to go wrong, you know."

"You run through it," said Alex. "I'm going down to the cafeteria to get some coffee."

"Better not put anything on that little shelf under the computer table," I whispered to Alex. "I wouldn't want you to get brained during the demo."

"When would you want me to get brained?" he whispered back. "I won't put anything there that I'll need during the show."

We all went down to the cafeteria to get some coffee. Then we all went back up to the roof and looked at the empty space again. Then we all went back down to my office and milled around. At nine o'clock, when most sensible people arrived at work, the sensible people from DoTI's graphics department walked into my office and asked where we wanted them to put the mockup.

Delamain volunteered to show the way. Stevie and Ben went along to help. Don, Alex, and I emitted a collective whoosh of relief and my phone started ringing.

By 10 o'clock the program was set. None of the visitors would be here for lunch. Cancel that. The NASA administrator would arrive in the Secretary's office at 1:30. The Hill would be there at 2:00. At 2:30 Hump (where on earth was he?) would go down to the Secretary's office and escort the entire herd to the roof (without rehearsal could he find the roof?). Delamain would greet them there and show them to their assigned spots.

At 11 o'clock John lurched into my office. "Steve and Ben are still working on the mockup. We'll eat lunch in shifts. Where's Hump?"

Don came in on his heels. "Probably chasing his damned dog."

"I'd be willin' to take his place if he doesn't get here in time." Lee Roy. "I mean, somebody's gonna have to do it."

"I'm familiar with the speech, Lee Roy," John said. "But thanks, anyway."

"Well, I don't like givin' speeches, but I'll do it." Lee Roy was all heart. "You'll be busy with your tinker toy, Clyde."

"When's lunch?" And there was Hump in all his fat grandeur.

I briefed him quickly on the arrangements. "Good. We're all set, then."

"Your speech, Hump. We still have time for me to help you rehearse."

Hump glared at John. "I looked the 3x5s over on the plane. I think you've helped enough. I'm going to get something to eat and then I'm going to go over the outline. I don't want to be disturbed. I'll see you on the roof." Hump shuffled off to his office.

Ben walked in. "Will someone else go up and help Steve with the mockup? The DoTI people don't have it placed exactly right and it's too heavy for him to move by himself. We got cold up there and decided to take turns working on it. Steve sent me out to launch early. He'll come down to the cafeteria when he starts to turn blue and I'll trade places with him."

"Since Hump thinks he doesn't need me, I'll go." John headed for the door. "I want to make sure everything is in the right place, anyway."

"Hokay. Steve said I should ask whoever goes up to stop in Steve's office and get his briefcase and jacket. He's turning blue."

Delamain nodded. "I'd better get my coat, too." He trotted off.

Lee Roy got up. "Well, since Delamain is busy bein' an errand boy, I think I'll go up and keep Chandler company. If he's movin' props around, I might even get to see him split them tight-assed britches of his. Besides, I wouldn't mind fiddlin' with that mockup myself."

"Well then," said Ben, "send Steve down to join me in the cafeteria now. We can't all be Fiddlers on the Roof, you know."

And finally it was 2:30.

March 9, 1990

I was shivering up there on the roof, wedged between Don and Lee Roy in the space allotted to the non-performing members of the Laboratory for Industrial Technology staff. We were all a little nervous, all very chilly. That ass Delamain kept mumbling about how nice and brisk it was.

Our group was situated on the near left of the stairs coming up. The Members of the Subcommittee stood toward the far left, joined by the Subcommittee staff and the Department of Trade and Industry's Congressional liaison. The NASA brass and the DoTI dignitaries were at the far right. I glanced over at the Subcommittee. Congressman Jaeklin seemed impervious to the chill. Good. I sneaked a peak at the Department's delegation. The Secretary looked frozen and murderous. Not good.

In the no-man's land between the Congress and the Executive, Hump was peering over his belly at the stack of 3x5 crib cards we had prepared for him.

Don nudged me. "If the wind blows those cards out of his hands, we're dead."

Lee Roy leaned over. "Whad'd you say, Clyde?"

Me. “Shhhh.”

Hump was standing within a cut-away mockup of a space vehicle. DoTI's graphics department had done a superb job. The controls looked realistic, the 'hull' was heavy enough to withstand the occasional windy blasts, and the scale was big enough to comfortably hold Hump. I had the feeling that a real spacecraft cabin would have fit him like a sausage casing. As it was, he looked impressive -- framed nicely by the open door, the Washington Monument at a distance behind him.

At the near left of the roof, Alex was checking the cables to his micro. One last check. One last prayer. At the other end of the cables, in the center of the roof, were the robot arms; next to them was a table laden with various objects; at the far center left, a stool.

Hump cleared his throat loudly and began his speech. "I would like to thank you all for coming here when I know there are warmer, more comfortable places you would like to be. But we thought that you would -- well, never mind that". He turned to the next card.

Steve winced.

"Robot arms are essential to the performance of many tasks, uh, many tasks performed by our astronauts, who, uh, perform many tasks at a distance and require robot arms. Sofar, these arms have been single arms, each programmed to, uh, perform individual tasks. Devising a way to get two or more arms to work together has been a very stubborn problem -- a problem that NASA had been unable to solve -- at least until they came to my lab."

I looked over at the gaggle of Executive dignitaries. Now the NASA Administrator looked murderous.

Hump grinned. "When the two-armed robots go up in a spacecraft, they will be driven by much more sophisticated software than what we have here. And there won't be all these cables around for the astronauts to trip over. But the hard work has been done, and the rest is up to NASA. Turn it on, Alex." Hump put the unread cards in his jacket pocket and folded his arms across his paunch.

Alex typed the robot's name, 'Tarzan', onto the keyboard. The micro whirred, the cables transmitted the commands and the robot arms swung toward the table. One arm picked up a glass jar. The other arm moved in and deftly untwisted the cap. The arms set the jar and cap gently down on the table. Congressman Jaeklin applauded.

Unnoticed by the multitude, Alex made an 'aw, it was nuthin' gesture. He really was cute.

Now the arms swung toward their next task - the stool. Abruptly, they paused, changed direction, and accelerated toward the figure standing at the edge of the roof.

I closed my eyes. Opened them again. *Oh, my God, no! Stop!*

At the computer terminal, Alex frantically punched at the keys.

But Tarzan had reached his destination. The little robot arm unflexed and pushed.

The Hill delegation, the NASA brass, the DoTI dignitaries, Alex and the rest of our LIT staff -- we all stood, paralyzed. Then a stampede toward the cut-away mockup where Hump no longer stood. Congressman Jaeklin got there first. He looked over the edge to the pavement six stories below. "Oh, shit," he said.

PART II

THE EXECUTABLE FILE

the assembled program that contains

the code for the execution

CHAPTER 10

March 9 (cont.) - 12, 1990

Lenore began screaming and hurled herself into the arms of the nearest male. Stevie. He ineffectually patted her shoulder while trying to hand her off to the next nearest male -- Delamain -- who didn't want her, either.

Then the LIT security guards burst onto the roof; I haven't the faintest idea how they were summoned. Somehow, they managed to herd us quickly into the third floor auditorium while they - or someone -- decided what to do with that high-ranking mess. The groups, which had become scrambled during the panic on the roof, re-sorted themselves into corners of the big room. The Hill, the Executive, the LIT staff -- each in its own huddled bunch -- like ethnics in their self-made ghettos.

"Don, where's Alex?"

"He's still on the roof with some of the security guards. They're gonna need him to figure out what happened."

"What did happen?" Ben was struggling out of his coat. The auditorium was considerably warmer than the roof. "Robots don't just go off on their own."

"Who's in charge here? These security flunkies can't handle this." Stevie was struggling to keep his voice from breaking. "I'll go back up and try to help."

"Do that," commanded Delamain. "I suppose the police have been called. They'll tell us all to go home as soon as they're satisfied it was an accident."

"The D.C. police? This is a Federal building," Don said. "Isn't it some Fed force like the FBI or the Secret Service? What difference does it make, anyway? Christ!"

Ben the Meticulous said, "This is an overlapping jurisdiction between the D.C .police and the FBI, which has charge of Government Reservations - we're one of those. Unless something involving national security happens, the FBI will probably let the D.C. police handle it."

I couldn't help it; I was curious. "Why do they call the Federal buildings Government Reservations?"

"Because," Ben said, "there are too many Chiefs." He looked across at Delamain.

There was nothing we could say after that, so we sat for a while, saying nothing.

I was unable even to think of anything except Alex. Then I found myself thinking about not thinking of anything except Alex.

"We're gonna have to get us a new Director." Lee Roy apparently had been thinking.

"The Secretary's over there." Don gestured toward the far corner of the auditorium. "Why don't you just go over and apply, jerk?"

Lee Roy grinned. "I might just do that, Clyde, I might just do that." He settled more comfortably in his seat and began whistling softly. 'Behold the Lord High Executioner'.

Don stared at him. "If you whistle, sing, hum, or mention that song in front of Alex, I'll break both of your kneecaps."

Lee Roy grinned. "Well, well. I sorta thought LuLuBelle was sweet on the guy, Clyde. I didn't know he was your type, too."

Don glowered.

Ben said, "Who's going to tell Mauve? She'd better not hear about this on tv."

The man was right. "I don't know what the protocol is. Should it be done out of the Secretary's office? Does anyone at LIT know Mauve well?"

"I do," Lee Roy said, "but I sure don' wanna be the one to tell her. Whyn't I go over and ask the Secretary?"

"No." John was firm. "With Hump gone, I'm ranking. I'll ask him." Delamain bustled off.

Steve rejoined us with the news that they weren't letting anyone up on the roof.

A large man in a blue uniform with a great deal of gold trim mounted the steps to the stage. He tapped on the microphone, bringing a sudden hush to the auditorium. "Thank you for your patience, ladies and gentlemen. We have obtained a list of all of your names from the LIT secretary and, should anything unexpected arise from further investigation, we may contact any or all of you. In the meantime, I can tell you that this appears to have been a tragic accident and we would like to extend our sincere condolences to all of Mr. Stafford's colleagues. We will be closing the building for the remainder of the day. You may return to your jobs on Monday."

It took a minute or two before we realized that we had been told to go home. There was a rush for the door.

I gathered up the necessaries from my office and walked down toward Alex's lab. The halls were full of techies, eager for information. Unfortunately, I didn't have any beyond the bare bones of what had happened and the news that we were all to go home until Monday.

Eventually, I reached the lab. Alex wasn't there. I repeated my broken field run back up toward the roof, but was stopped by a uniformed guard stationed at the staircase.

"I'm looking for Dr. Carfil."

"There's no one on the roof now except some of our people, ma'am."

"Do you know where he is?"

"No ma'am."

I left the building and went home. About six o'clock, I phoned Alex's house. No answer. No point in calling LIT -- the switchboard was unattended. No answer at Alex's at eight, ten, or midnight. I filled in the time looking at television. The news broadcasts were full of the killer robot, run amok. Finally, I fell asleep watching the Late Show, or the Late Late Show, or something like that.

I tried Alex again in the morning, still without result. At 9:30 on the head, Don called. Connie must have made him wait for a decent hour to phone. He didn't want anything in particular, just to talk. "What do you think this is going to do to LIT?"

"Haven't the foggiest. I suppose it will depend on who the new Director is. And whether they find out why Tarzan turned homicidal. What are you going to do, Don?"

"Wait and see who we get for a Director. If it's Delamain, I'm going to try to bail out. What about you?"

"The same. I'd like to continue working with you."

"Let's try. We're both liable to be pariahs after this, though."

"Too true. I've been trying to find Alex. Have you heard from him?"

"Uh uh. Do you have his home number?"

"Yeah. He doesn't answer. I was going to wait until noon and then drive over to see if he's there and just not answering."

"Let me know if you find him. Bea, was Lee Roy's shot in the dark on target?"

"You mean am I 'sweet on' Alex? I guess you could say that."

"He's a good guy. Well, let me know." Don hung up.

Noon came and I drove over to Alex's. He wasn't there. The little house was locked up tight. I drove over to LIT. Also locked up tight and with security guards at all the doors. Polite, but adamant. No admittance.

Saturday passed, and Sunday. From time to time, I'd flip on the tv set. The Saturday news broadcasts were crammed with horror stories of killer robots. The talk show hosts grilled innumerable computer scientists who spewed immeasurable nonsense. By Sunday, both the coverage and the nonsense had tapered off.

The hours of waiting and worrying were broken every once in while by calls from Don, from Ben, from Stevie, even from Hope Lahti and Freddie Langsteth. They had no more of a clue than I as to what this meant for LIT.

Inevitably, Monday arrived. I drove to the office early, not for any reason except that I was sick of being at home. I dropped my briefcase in my office and went down to Alex's lab.

Alex was there. He was sitting at his desk. He turned as I came in.

Alex looked as if he hadn't slept since Friday. His tousled hair was more tousled; his face was pale; his eyes bloodshot. He may have spent some time crying.

I started to go to him but he shook his head. I stopped.

"Oh, my dear, where have you been?"

"Here. I stayed with the police investigating team Friday night and just didn't go home. I must have run Tarzan a hundred times. It does what it's supposed to do. Bea, what am I going to do? My career is finished. LIT will never come through this. The whole robotics program may be dead. And I killed a man. Not bad going for an obscure Government computernik."

He smiled wryly. "I was going to ask you to marry me, Bea. Not right away, you know, but soon. Oh, God."

I sat down. "When you get around to it, I'll accept. Alex, your career matters to me only because it matters to you. I'd marry you if you were a used car salesman." I thought for a minute. "Well, maybe a new car salesman. LIT's important, but if we don't do the job, someone else will be given the responsibility. The function won't be abandoned. The robotics program may be delayed but it won't stop. And you didn't kill Hump."

"Tarzan was my baby."

"Alex, stop it! I don't know anything about computers except that they don't do anything they aren't told to do. And unless you told Tarzan to murder Hump, you aren't responsible for what happened."

"That's just it, Bea. It couldn't have happened. It just couldn't have happened."

"Then someone else told Tarzan to do it."

"How?" he said, simply.

"How the hell do I know? You're the technical genius; you figure it out." And finally, I went to him.

We stayed in an embrace for some time, not saying anything. Finally, I disengaged. "I'd better get upstairs."

"Will you come back later?"

I nodded and left.

The hall was filled with knots of arriving staffers, still with their coats on. Whispering and wondering. LIT wasn't going to get much work done.

There was a note on my desk from Lenore. "Mr. Delamain has called a staff meeting in the Director's conference room at 9:30." Mr. Delamain. Did Lenore know something I didn't know? Something extremely unpleasant?

I stopped at Stevie's office on my way to the conference room. He was on the phone with his broker. "I tell ya it's O.K. I'll cover the goddam margin. Gimme until tomorrow morning. No problem, guy." He looked up and saw me, gestured to a chair. To the broker. "We got it made. Stick with Steve. Gi' my love to Cleo."

Three things are certain. Death, taxes, and Stevie's dealies.

Steve hung up. "Have you heard anything?"

"Zip. Damned if I can see how it happened."

Stevie shook his head. "Terrible. Maybe Alex can figure it out. I suppose the best thing for us to do is just carry on. Whoever the new Director is'll have a hard enough time without the routine going to hell." He paused a minute. "Any word on who's gonna take over?"

"Not a clue. I suppose Delamain will be Acting until they pick someone. At least he thinks so. He's called a staff meeting. Were you invited?"

Steve laughed. "Yeah. Delamain'll keep inviting me until he finds out you lied about me knowing a senator. Is it time?"

He got up and we walked to the meeting together.

Lenore snorfed at us as we passed. "Well, there are certainly going to be some changes made now."

I tried to snorf back -- unsuccessfully as always. "There already have been."

Stevie smiled innocently. "Better start updating your personnel form, Lenore. I'll help you if you like."

"Why should I do that?"

"Well, I suppose any new Director would bring his own secretary."

Lenore paled and we boogied on.

Don, John, and Lee Roy were already in the room. John was at the head of the table.

"As the highest ranking SESer, I'll be Acting Director, at least until a regular appointment is made."

"You countin' chickens, Clyde? You're never gonna get that job."

"I suppose you think you are?"

"Stranger things, Clyde, stranger things."

I wondered if Lee Roy had some inside information. God forbid. Don whispered to me, "Can you see either of those clowns surviving the confirmation hearing?"

I had forgotten that the Director of LIT was a Presidential appointment and therefore subject to Congressional confirmation. I had a sudden antic vision of Lee Roy in the hearing room.

From the Chairman: "Tell me, Mr. Dubble, do you think you can get to the bottom of that tragic affair of the robot?"

From Lee Roy: "Well, Clyde, if you ast me..."

A bellow, "Don't call me Clyde, goddammit." I looked up, startled. The bellow had come from Delamain.

Lee Roy cackled. "Whatever you say, Slick."

The door opened and Lenore came in. "The Secretary's office just called, Mr. Delamain. Professor Lee will be here tomorrow at 9:00 for the briefing. The Secretary would like you to come down half an hour before Professor Lee's arrival for a short meeting with the Secretary and his staff and then stay to greet the Professor. After that, you will escort him up here for the briefing."

Lenore smiled smarmily at Stevie and me and departed.

John squared his shoulders. "Well, you heard that. I must say that they might have waited a bit, out of respect for poor Hump. We'll use the large conference room, I think. Bea, would you ask Alex to be there at 9:30? Perhaps he can tell the Professor what went wrong."

How come John didn't want to give *that* presentation?

"Oh, and I think it would be best if you all called me 'Mr. Delamain'. Only in public, of course. In our own councils, you may continue to call me John. After Professor Lee's visit, I shall want to talk with each of you individually, so please hold tomorrow free. That will be all for now."

John gathered his papers and sailed out.

"Well, Clyde," Stevie said to Lee Roy, "I think we're all in the shit, but your shit is the shittiest." Stevie left, followed by a subdued Lee Roy.

I spent the rest of the day coping with phone calls.

At 5:00 I went down to collect Alex, threading my way through the still-milling staff. Alex looked a little better.

I kissed him on the nose. "You want to go out to eat or come over to my house for dinner? I think my refrigerator will run to a couple of steaks."

Alex put on his coat. "Would it be too much trouble if we went to your house?"

"Let's go."

We got my car. Despite the fact that Alex seemed to be recovering, I wasn't at all sure that he was fit to drive. "There's a Professor Lee, from MIT, arriving at LIT tomorrow for a briefing. Delamain wants you in the main conference room at 9:30."

"Oh, no. Is this an official inquiry?"

"I shouldn't think so. They were trying to get a delegation from MIT here for the demo but there was a schedule mismatch. I think this is just a leftover."

"Oh. O.K. Who's Lee?"

"I don't know. My notes just say that his first name is Philip. The only academic Lee that I know is a biologist from Cal Tech. P.I. Lee. I never knew his real first name, which is odd, now that I think of it. He and his wife were old friends of Harry's parents and they were like family to us. We called them Uncle Pie and Aunt Bessie. They would have been our baby's godparents. I lost contact with them after Harry died."

Alex put his arm around me. "What did you do, Bea, crawl in a hole?"

"I guess so. Yeah. For the first few months, it just hurt too much to see anyone. Particularly people that Harry and I were close to, people we loved. After the hurt wore off a little, it was just too...awkward, I suppose. I don't know. I'd rejected offers of comfort and that must have been hard for people like Pie and Bessie. I didn't know what to do after that."

Alex squeezed my shoulder.

As we sat eating Alex said, "Bea, do you really want to marry me?"

"Are you really proposing?"

Alex nodded. "I love you. But I want you to be sure that this isn't just part of your process of climbing out of a hole. Are you sure it's not that?"

"Yes. I've thought about it, Alex. There's no getting around the fact that you're sexy. Thoughts of copulation crossed my mind the first time I walked into your office."

Alex grinned. "We do think a lot alike."

I pitched a breadstick at him. "There's also no getting around the fact that I'm lonesome. Three years alone is a long three years. Until Friday, I wasn't really sure that my feelings for you weren't just a combination of adolescent passion and a need for someone, anyone."

"And apart from the memorable event on the roof," Alex asked, "what happened Friday?"

I reached over and took his hand. "When we were waiting in the auditorium, I should have thought about a lot of things. The future of LIT. My career. How Mauve was going to take it. But the only thing I really worried about -- cared about -- was you and what this would do to us. I loved Harry and I love you."

We washed the dishes and we made love and we didn't think of Tarzan or Hump or that ass Delamain. Life with Alex was certainly having its moments.

CHAPTER 11

March 13, 1990

I grabbed the alarm clock before it woke Alex. I was dipping the French toast when I heard his familiar off-key warble emanating from the shower. My Wand'ring Minstrel had arisen. He wandered into the kitchen, barefoot, rubbing his head with a towel. Another towel was draped precariously around his waist.

Alex grabbed me and kissed me soundly on the back of my neck. This proved too much for his sarong, which floated ignominiously to the floor. The two of us stood there snickering like fools.

"Bea, do you have a razor?"

"Only a ladies' electric." I stood back and regarded his three-day growth of stubble. "I don't think it will make it."

"Maybe I should grow a beard. I may need a disguise, anyway."

"Have some French toast."

Alex rearranged his towel and sat down. "You know," he said, "I really don't know very much about you."

"I would have thought that after last night you knew as much as you'll ever need to know."

"C'mon, Bea. You know what I mean. Tell me all about you."

"My life story over French toast? Not very interesting, I'm afraid. I was a change-of-life baby – Mom and Pop were both in their 50's when I was born -- an only child. So I was sort of brought up by people who might have been my grandparents. They were both immigrants from somewhere in central Europe and they immigrated without the rest of their families. So the three of us were pretty much alone.

"But it wasn't a bad childhood. We lived in a lower middle class neighborhood in Chicago. I had a circle of friends – all of whom I've lost track of – so I wasn't lonely and Mom used to shlep me off to museums so I even had something of an intellectual life. And, of course, there were the pigeons."

"Oh yes, of course," Alex muttered, "the pigeons. What pigeons?"

I chortled. "We rented a flat in a two-family house. It had a garage. Over the garage our landlord had built a pigeon coop, in which he had about 60 pigeons."

"What did he do with them? Eat them?"

"My God, no! They were sort of pets. I think he belonged to a club where they raced them."

"I see," said Alex, who didn't look like he saw at all.

"Anyway" I went on, "inside the garage there was a primitive ladder which allowed both my landlord and Mrs. Peterson's cat to enter the coop."

"I see," said Alex again, "Mrs. Peterson's cat. Did the cat eat the pigeons?"

"She tried. The Petersons lived two doors down and they could see into our yard from their place. As could the cat - a big orange beast. Every once in a while the cat would creep over to our garage, sneak up the ladder, and arrive in the pigeon coop."

"And ate a pigeon or two?"

"One cat is no match for 60 pigeons. The cat would enter. The pigeons would fly up from their roosts and frantically beat their wings. It being a relatively constrained space, many of these very powerful wings would land on the cat, beating the bejesus out of her. She'd slink down the ladder and creep back to her own yard."

"Didn't that dissuade her from returning to the coop?"

"Not for long. For the first week or so she'd lick her wounds and look everywhere except toward the coop. Then gradually her wounds would heal and you could almost hear her thinking. 'Cats don't get beat up by birds. Cats catch birds and eat them. I am a cat. Therefore, I never got the bejesus beat out of me by some birds and I will go eat them.' And thewhole scene would play out again. The cat never learned. Reminds me of the U.S. Congress."

Alex laughed. "Go on with the main narrative."

"Well, just about the time I was ready to enter college, my folks died. Mom from complications from diabetes and Pop from a heart attack. They were both around 70 and in that era, it wasn't considered an untimely death."

I looked at my watch. "We'd better get licking. I'll continue this fascinating tale later."

"Did you keep any of Harry's underwear? My stuff is a little gamey."

I handed Alex the honey. "Why would I keep underwear? A fetishist I ain't. We can stop at your house on the way to the office and you can make yourself presentable. Let's move it. Lee will be there at nine."

"I thought you said 9:30."

"That's when you arrive."

"Ah. Bea, I figured out how it could have been done."

"How?"

Alex swallowed his toast. "I'll tell you in the car. We'd better run."

We were out of the house and on our way to Alex's by 7:30.

"Alex, why didn't Tarzan stop when you hit the Cancel key? You did hit the Cancel key?"

"I damn near pushed it through the floor. Tarzan has a buffer memory that stores commands. When you put in the instructions, they get held in the buffer until they're executed. You can't cancel until the buffer is empty. There was enough stored to push Hump off the roof. We won't use the buffer when Tarzan gets into space, but it was the easiest way to operate for now.

"Can I tell you the hard part now?"

"Tell."

"I'm going to go over some ground you already know, but I think it'll help you to keep it straight. Bear with me. Tarzan's brain is a computer program that gives his arms instructions. Now that program is, essentially, a code which is stored on a hard disk attached to my microcomputer. There are a lot of other programs, which have nothing to do with Tarzan, also stored on that hard disk. Each one of those programs has a unique name, which is entered in a directory that I can have displayed on the screen when I want to see what's on the disk. That's in case I forget what I've got on there. When I want to use one of the programs that I've stored, I just type the name on the computer's keyboard. You with me?"

"I'm with you."

"O.K. Now, there are two ways to get something onto my micro's hard disk. One way is to sit at the key-board and type whatever you want and then tell the computer to save it on the hard disk. The other way is to use a keyboard on a compatible machine and type the program onto a floppy disk. Then you can take the floppy disk, put it in one of my micro's disk drives, and use the keyboard to tell the computer to copy the program from the floppy onto the hard disk. You can do whatever you want with the floppy after that. Still with me?"

"Still with you."

We arrived at Alex's house and ran inside while he shaved and changed. We were out and on our way to the office by 8:15.

"Give me the next installment."

"What could have happened is that someone copied the Tarzan program from my hard disk to a floppy. Did I tell you that you can copy in either direction?"

"No, but I knew it. Would there be enough room on a floppy to contain your whole program?"

"Yeah. Eventually, when all of the wrinkles are added, a floppy won't hold it. But right now, yeah.

"Anyway, once the bad guy copies it from my hard disk to his floppy, he has a copy of my program. Then all he has to do is doctor it. He finds the instruction that tells the arms to start moving toward the stool, then he erases it and all the succeeding instructions and substitutes his instructions for the murder. If he doctored the floppy in advance, and I think he must have, he doesn't know exactly where Stafford will be standing, but he does know that there will be an exact spot."

I nodded. "Right. Delamain had everything except the mockup set days in advance."

"So what the bad guy does, is write in a 'place saver' that will have to be changed at the last minute when he knows exactly where Stafford will stand."

"And this program tells Tarzan to push Hump off the roof?

"You got it."

I shook my head. "Then why didn't Tarzan push when you re-ran the program?"

"What I think the bad guy did was to write a 'kamikaze' program and load it onto my hard disk just before the demo."

"Huh?"

"Look. You remember that you have to give every program a unique name?"

"Yep."

"Well, you can also rename a program. So what the bad guy has to do is name his program 'Tarzan', just like mine. Let me give it to you in steps. First, he copies Tarzan onto a floppy disk and takes it home so he can work on it in peace. Because the original Tarzan is left sitting on the hard disk, I'd never know that someone had been at it. Second, he doctors the version on the floppy, putting in an instruction to 'push' at an arbitrary coordinate. Third, after the mock-up is in place he figures out the coordinate where Hump will be standing. Fourth, he finds the place on the impostor program where the coordinate where Hump will be. Fifth, he changes the name of my Tarzan to something else -- 'Jane', for instance. O.K. so far?"

"Keep going."

"Now the last two instructions in the bad guy's program are to change the name 'Jane' back to 'Tarzan' and erase his program. In other words, the program commits suicide. Then when I run Tarzan again, nothing happens that shouldn't happen. Follow?"

I thought for a while. "I think so. How the hell are we ever going to prove it?"

I drove into the parking lot. It was 8:35.

Alex kissed me. "Let's talk about it this afternoon. There's gotta be a way."

I dealt with the mail, sorted the phone messages into priority order, and stuck my head into the reception room. "Is the meeting still scheduled for nine?" There was small likelihood that Lenore would have alerted me to a cancellation.

"It's still on. Although Mr. Delamain says he will probably reconstitute the staff after this. It's really too bad that you're not technical. I can't imagine where LIT can use you." She started to say something else and stopped.

"Did you want something, Lenore?"

"No. I just wondered if you knew what was going to happen to Dr. Schnabel."

"I have no idea. I'm not sure that a new Director can stop the process once it gets to the Inspector General. Assuming that a new Director would want to."

Lenore donned her sanctimonious look. "Well, I don't think it should be stopped. The man is no better than a common thief." Snorf. "But maybe he's suffered enough for his crimes. He looked just terrible when I saw him last Friday."

"You saw Gus on Friday? Here?"

"On the third floor, going into the Inspector General's office. Listen, Bea, I don't have time to gossip anymore."

Lenore turned to her word processor and I mooched off to the conference room. I sat down next to Don. "Has John been anointed yet?"

Don shook his head. "Not that I know of."

The door of the conference room opened and Delamain appeared. He looked pale and unhappy. "Gentlemen and lady," he said, "I have the honor of presenting LIT's new Acting Director, Dr. Philip Lee."

John entered the room followed by a tall, late middle-aged, distinguished-looking Eurasian. Namely, Uncle Pie.

Professor P.I. Lee is a biologist of considerable stature; a member of the National Academy of Sciences; chairman of the President's Commission on Scientific Exchange with the People's Republic of China; recipient of the Biotechnology Society Pioneer Award; and, I'm sure, a pocketful of other honors collected during the three years that I had lost sight of him. He was also a marvelous guy. One of the few genuinely funny people whose humor has no trace of cruelty about it. When Harry and I were married, it was Uncle Pie who gave me away.

Uncle Pie was the product of a Chinese mathematician father and a Brooklyn Jewish housewife mother. His erect figure was always impeccably swathed. His shoes shone with an enviable luster. His ties were muted and silk. And he had an absolutely outlandish Brooklyn accent.

Pie was married to Aunt Bessie, a smiling little lady who was a dead ringer for the rebitzim who grace Sholem Aleichem's tales of Jewish life in the Ukraine. Aunt Bessie did all the traditional things. She made latkes. She cleaned house with a single-minded fury. She arranged Seders and was the arranging genius behind countless marriages. She was also the world-renowned archeologist, Dr. Elizabeth Lee. It was Aunt Bessie who had inspired Harry in his choice of a career.

"Dr. Lee," John said, "I would like to introduce LIT's senior staff. Mr. Lee Roy Dubble, who was one of Mr. Stafford's close advisors. Mr. Donald Cromarty, our Director of Operations. Mr. Stephen Chandler, our Executive Officer. And last, but not least, our Senior Economist, Dr. Beatrice Goode."

"Young fella," said Pie, grinning like a lunatic, "I don't need an introduction to Bea Goode. Baby, how are ya?" He bounded over and pinched my cheeks.

I kissed him. "I was great until you demolished my face."

"I got a million things to tell ya, but let's get this meeting out of the way first. Where's the fella with the two-armed robot?"

John was desperately trying to hang on to the tatters of decorum. "He is due to arrive at 9:30."

"O.K. So *nu*? We got fifteen minutes to get acquainted before he gets here." Pie sat down across from me, leaving the head-of-the-table to John.

"I'm the boss, so I'll talk. My name is P.I. Lee but everyone calls me Pie. Not the Greek letter -- I'm not a mathematician. I'm a biologist so they call me something organic, like a dessert. Your last -- late -- Director was a computer fella, so of course LIT's scientific emphasis was on computers. I'm a biologist, so you can probably figure out that the emphasis is going to change a little. Don't any of you worry about it. I'm not going to do anything in a hurry and nobody'll get hurt, if I can help it. Obviously, as an organization, the first thing we've got to do is find out what caused that terrible tragedy on Friday. As I said, I'm not a computer guy so I'm not going to be able to give you much technical help. But I'll try to get you the resources you need for the investigation. To tell you the truth, I don't think money is the resource you need for that. I think you need time more than anything else and my job is to buy you that time. Did Stafford do all the dealing with the Hill or does one of you do it?"

I raised my hand.

"Fine, then we got something else to talk about after this meeting."

The door opened and Lenore came in.

"Dr. Carfil is here, Dr. Lee."

Pie got up and went to the door. "C'mon in."

He clapped Alex on the shoulder. "Sit down. I read the summary of what your robot was supposed to do. Did it ever actually take the wheels off that toy truck?"

"Yes, sir."

"Call me Pie."

Alex gaped, and for a minute I thought he was going to blurt out "Uncle Pie!". As it was, all he said was, "O.K."

"That's a hell of an accomplishment, kid. Do you know what went wrong?"

"I'm beginning to get an idea but I haven't worked it out yet."

"What do you need?"

"Time."

"What else?"

"The equipment is still on the roof. We've been lucky that it hasn't rained. The security man told me that they were going to lift the guard today and take the stuff inside. I'd like it left up there where I can play with it. Could we keep the roof closed off to everyone except me and a tent put up to protect the equipment?"

"O.K. Who takes care of details like that?"

"Lenore can do it," I said. "Do you want me to tell her?"

"Yeh. Better get it done now."

I went out to Lenore's desk. "Lenore, would you call Security and have the roof entrances padlocked and a key given to Dr. Carfil and no one else. And call Property and have them put a tent over the whole shebang right away."

"Listen, Bea, I have to get the mail..."

The conference room door opened and Pie erupted. He swatted me on the fanny. "Hey, Lenore -- that's your name, isn't it?"

"Yes, sir."

"I've got reservations on NYAir to Boston tonight. Get them changed to the first flight out tomorrow. But do Bea's stuff first." He kissed me on the cheek. "Boy, is it good to see you again."

We went back into the conference room, leaving a shell-shocked Lenore.

Pie settled himself again. "It's about 10:30 now." Turning to Alex. "You want to cut out and get to work?"

"Unless you need me."

"Naw. Go to it. If anything significant turns up today, ring right through to me. If not, give Bea a progress report at the end of every day. You don't have to write it out, just tell her. She's as much of a technical lox as I am, so if she understands it, so will I. But don't talk to anyone else about it, just Bea.

"Bea, if Carfil tells you anything that sounds significant, call me at home in Boston. Don't you talk about it to anyone else either. I think that's the most efficient use of our time. Carfil won't have to waste his time writing and the two of us can stay up to speed. If you think that something needs more explanation than you can give, Carfil can get on the phone too. O.K.?"

Alex and I nodded, and he left.

"Now the rest of you four fellas. I want an hour and a half with each of you this afternoon, starting at 1:30. What I want you to do is write a list of everything you've got under your wings and then I want you to give me a quick oral briefing on the whole bag. You'll each have at least three hours to prepare. I can get written follow-ups next week, when we've got more time. Who wants to be first?"

John was clearly unhappy. "Pie, I've been extremely busy this past week and I'm a bit behind on my own briefings..."

"How much of your stuff are you on top of?"

"It's not that I'm not on top of everything, I'm just not absolutely current."

"So *nu*? How much are you not absolutely current on?"

"I'd say about half."

"O.K., you got a forty-five minute appointment. Send up the guys who would normally brief you, and they can fill in the other forty-five."

"Pie, I really must protest. You've never been in Government before and I don't think you realize how important chain-of-command is. Dr. Carfil really should not go outside of the chain-of-command to report to Bea. That is very bad for morale, very bad."

Don leaned over and whispered, "Whose morale?"

Delamain wasn't finished. "And the technical staff should not brief you directly, outside of my presence. Once you establish that kind of precedent, they'll pester you to death. You won't have a minute to do your important work."

"You don't think talking to the technical staff is important?" Pie shrugged. "Listen, young fella, LIT's got a budget of about six million bucks and under 200 staff members including all the clericals, right?"

Delamain nodded.

"This is a little outfit with a big job. My senior staff should have more important things to do besides Mickey Mousing around playing gate-keeper. Now you may be right and I may live to regret this. But right now we'll do it my way. Go tell your people that I want to see them starting at 2:15. I'll see you at 1:30. Since you've only got half a briefing to prepare, you go first."

John picked up his briefcase and left, lips compressed.

"Who wants three o'clock?"

"I can take it," Stevie said.

"Naw," said Don. "You've got the details. I think it would be better if I gave Pie the budget overview first so he knows what you're talking about." He turned to Pie. "Unless you want us together."

"No. You're right, though. Chandler should come after you." Don nodded. "Bea can brief you on a lot of my stuff better than I can." He turned to me. "If you take the tech assessments, the status at OMB, and the Hill, I'll cover the Export Committee, the industry support campaign, and the status in the Department. I'll let Lenore know where I am when you're talking to Pie, and you do the same when I'm on the grill. That way we can bail one another out if we have to."

Pie laughed. "Now you're talkin'. O.K. You at three. Chandler at 4:30." To Steve. "Will you need an hour and a half?"

"I don't think so. Forty-five minutes should do it."

Pie got to Lee Roy, who had been looking increasingly alarmed. "A quarter after five for you?"

Lee Roy nodded.

"That's it, then. I hadn't planned to join LIT until June, so I've still got some thesis students to wrap up at MIT. The next couple of months'll be hairy. Bea, give me a half-hour to get my Boston schedule rearranged and then come on back here at 11:30. I'll get lunch sent up." Pie took leave. We could hear him telling Lenore to get some sandwiches for us at noon.

"Shee-it," said Lee Roy. "That old fart's gonna keep me here past my bedtime." Exit.

Don, Stevie, and I burst out laughing. "Looks like we got ourselves a Director," said Don. Exeunt.

As I approached Lenore's desk she asked, "What kind of sandwiches would you like, Bea? Will Swiss and ham be alright?"

"Fine, Lenore."

Stevie snickered and sauntered past.

"Lenore, is anyone doing anything about packing up Hump's things?"

"Well, I've thought about it. I suppose Dr. Lee will want that office, and I'd better get it ready for him."

"Someone should go through the stuff and separate Hump's personal belongings from the official stuff. And bring his personal things over to Mauve. Unless Mauve wants to do the sort."

Lenore thought. "I could call her and ask. If she doesn't want to do it, and I honestly don't think she will, should I sort the stuff?"

Times had certainly changed. "I think that would be best. If there's something that isn't obviously personal or official, feel free to ask me or Don."

She nodded. "But Bea, would you take the things over to Mauve? I don't think she likes me." Lenore sighed. "It's so often like that with the boss's wife and his secretary."

I smothered a giggle. "Of course. Let me know when the stuff has been sorted."

As I turned to leave, Frances Monk emerged from her office. "Bea, may I see you for a minute?"

I was flabbergasted. In the year I had been at LIT, our Chief Scientist had never spoken a direct word to me. It came as a surprise that she knew my name.

"Sure." I followed Monk into her office.

This was the first time that I had been in her office. The infamous 'classified' safe was against the wall, to the left of the door. Her desk, piled with reports, was against the left wall; on the right wall, a working table heaped with yet more reports; on the far wall, windows and file cabinets. A visitor's chair was plunked haphazardly between the desk and the table. Monk sank into her desk chair, motioned me to the visitor's chair.

We sat looking at each other for a while.

Finally, she said, "This isn't easy."

I nodded. "It isn't easy for me either. I've read about your career and what you've done in the computer field, and I feel as if I should salute. But that doesn't seem appropriate."

Monk smiled faintly. "That was a long time ago. Oh, I still know the words. Listen. 'Relational. Hierarchical. Network. Extract. Access and retrieval. Segmented. Slave. Query. Associative processors...'"

She went on, chanting jargon much as a schizophrenic tosses a word salad. At last she stopped.

"See? I can remember all that." She laughed grimly. "So can you, I bet. I need help, Bea."

An unworthy thought, "Why me?" Aloud, "What can I do?"

Monk got up and stood staring out the window. I glanced at the piles of reports on her desk. I could see none dated later than 1988. They were dusty.

She turned back. "That bitch from OPM knew what the score was. Chief Scientist like hell. Chief Boozer. She was going to see Hump, you know. I would've been downgraded, you know. Stafford wouldn't have helped me. Not him."

"Would that have been so terrible? You'd have kept your salary for three years."

Monk gave me a disgusted look. "And been put in an office to share with some kid in swaddling clothes." She glanced at her personal classified safe. "And sent to one damn A.A. group after another. And dumped in some velvet lined drunk tank and dried out. And after six months, canned. Oh, I know what would have happened. And don't say it, Bea, don't say it. I'm not hurting anyone the way I am. That's more than you can say for most people." She glanced at the safe again.

"I know what's in the safe. If you need a drink, take one."

Monk fiddled with the combination. "That's something else I remember. The numbers in the combination. Forget that and I'm done." She took out a bottle and a glass. "You want a belt?"

I shook my head. "Not now."

Monk knocked back damn near a tumblerful of gin, shuddered, and sat down. "I know what you're thinking. I know what happened to your husband. I hear things, you see. I hear lots of things. I don't drive, Bea." She looked at me earnestly. "I never drive. I take a cab to work. Don't own a car anymore. They didn't take away my license; I just decided not to drive. You see, I don't hurt anyone."

Abruptly, she stopped talking and sat staring at the dusty reports.

"What is it you want me to do, Dr. Monk?"

She roused herself.

"I saw you with the new Director. You know him. Tell him not to fire me. I don't hurt anyone. I'm no bother. All he has to do is have someone look in my office every day to see if I'm dead yet." She made a noise that might have been a laugh.

My God, what people do to themselves! "If you like. There may be a better way."

Monk raised an eyebrow.

"If you had enough money, say your retirement annuity plus a lump sum $35,000 to $50,000, would you rather retire?"

"You mean drink myself blind at home instead of here? Sure. You on good terms with the tooth fairy?"

"People get all sorts of awards for the things they don't do. You've never gotten one for the things you did do. I think a 'gold' carries almost $50,000 with it. I would never be party to one of those awards-for-bad-behavior, but I think you deserve some legitimate recognition for your contributions to the field."

How do you say things like that without sounding like a patronizing creep? God knows I didn't intend to patronize Frances Monk. "I'll give it a try if you want me to."

"Yes," said Monk, "yes." She stood up, holding herself rigidly straight. "That appears to be a very workable plan. I suggest we implement it forthwith."

I left that sad office. I heard the combination lock squeaking as I walked across the reception room.

How, I wondered, did Frances Monk ever get appointed as Chief Scientist of LIT? We were only a year old and she'd been pickled far longer than that. I bet myself a beagle to a bagel that the last guy she worked for recommended her highly for this job . Got her out of his hair, freed up a slot, and didn't have to go through all of the administrivia required to fire a drunk. Good move.

CHAPTER 12

March 13, 1990 (cont.)

Don was waiting for me when I got back to my office. "I take it you'd met our new Director before?"

"Uh huh." I explained.

"Bea, did you catch what he said about not expecting to be here until June?"

"Yeah. I guess Hump was on his way out."

Don nodded. "I wonder if he resigned or got canned."

"I don't know. And if it was a canning, I wonder if he knew it was coming."

"It would explain a few things if he did."

"Like why he decided to destroy poor Gus?"

"I wasn't thinking of that." Don looked puzzled. "What does Hump getting canned have to do with Gus?"

"Just to put a serious crimp in our software capability. And if he was mad enough, he might welcome leaving LIT with a scandal on its hands. I don't think any of us really knew him well enough to know whether he was a vengeful man. What did you have in mind?"

"A little matter of conflict-of-interest. The way he was acting about ZapaCall on the Export Committee. ZapaCall and DoTel are competitors. DoTel couldn't be happy about

ZapaCall getting a jump on exports. And that guy from DoTel was sure behaving as if he owned Hump. Do you think that fat bastard had himself set up for a job?"

I considered it. "It sure does fit the known facts."

I got up. "I'd better get to my meeting with Pie."

Pie was sitting at the conference room table when I came in. Impeccable, as always. Graying hair carefully combed. Tie in its proper place. Trousers sharply creased. Every inch the inscrutable Oriental. I burst into tears, and Pie jumped up from his chair and put his arms around me. I proceeded to blubber all over his English tweed jacket.

"Have you been waiting three years for this cry, Bea?"

I disengaged. "I'm not crying for Harry, Pie. I'm crying because I'm ashamed of myself. I've treated you and Bessie so badly. All I thought of was that I couldn't see anyone or talk to anyone, and I didn't think of you at all. Or the fact that you loved Harry, too. Or that you needed comfort."

I dug a Kleenex out of my pocket and, inelegantly, blew. "Fact is, this is the first time I've thought of that at all. I'm crying because I'm an insensitive...an insensitive..."

"*Schtunk,*" Pie supplied. "The word is *schtunk.*"

"Oh Pie, you always know just the right thing to say."

We both burst out laughing. "O.K.," he said, "if you're finished rending your garments, can we get down to business?"

"Alex and I are going to get married."

Pie sat down. "No kidding! That's great! My God, your Aunt Bessie'll *plotz.* Oi, she's in the Yucatan, digging. I can't tell her until she calls in. He's a smart guy. Is he as nice as he's smart? This is wonderful news. *Mazeltov.*"

"Thank you." I kissed him on his head.

Pie looked at me suspiciously. "You got any more bombshells, or can we start pretending that we work around here?"

"I'm all business, Pie."

"Awright. I know that I told the staff that I'm not going to do anything in a hurry, but I'm going to have to take some shortcuts. I suppose you've already figured out that Stafford's death was an on-purpose, not an accident."

"Alex and I have. I don't know about the rest of the staff."

"Yeah. Well, if he was murdered, someone murdered him and until we find out who did it, I don't trust anyone -- except you and that guy of yours. So I can't leave anyone in a position where they can find out how our investigation is going."

Our investigation. Pie, I love you. "Are you worried about Delamain being Acting Director when you're in Boston?"

"You got it. Is he as big an ass as I think he is?"

"Even without knowing how big an ass you think he is, I can answer, 'At least'."

"I figured. I don't know how the bureaucracy works. Can I do anything about it?"

I thought for a minute. "Yeah. You can give him a big, prestigious-sounding, harmless special assignment. Preferably one that involves travel."

"Can you think of one?"

"Why don't you take him to Boston with you? To give you an 'in-depth' briefing."

"*Gevalt*. You're fired. Think of something else, dummy."

"You're a hard man, Pie. Delamain doesn't know anything about biotech, and as Technical Director, he should. Do you have any friends at Cal Tech who owe you a favor?"

Pie contemplated. "A few. A few more who'd like to butter me up. What've you got in mind?"

"The best thing would be to find an immediate course on biotech someplace -- as a preference, Tanganyika -- and send him there. But assuming that we can't find a course to send him to, you could ship him off to Cal Tech right away for a couple of weeks of private tutorials. John is an ass, but he isn't a stupid ass. I think he's capable of assimilating a lot of information in a relatively short time, and I think LIT would benefit from having someone with a good conceptual grasp of both biotech and computer technology."

"I think you've got something. I'll set it up."

"Pie, I'm absolutely sure that Alex wasn't responsible for Hump's death. But I know the guy and I love him. Why are you so sure he had nothing to do with it?"

"You mean why am I trusting him with the investigation?"

I nodded.

"Because he's a smart fella. Dodos don't develop two-armed robots. And if he's a smart fella, he's not about to use a murder method that'd ruin his career. He woulda done something more subtle -- like brain the guy with a two by four."

The door opened and Lenore entered, laden with sandwiches. "I'll be right back with the beverage."

Pie looked at the six thick sandwiches on the platter. "How many of these things can you eat?"

"One."

Lenore came back in with a pot of coffee. "Lenore, take four of these sandwiches away and give them to someone else. Don't throw 'em out. Someone'll eat 'em."

"Is there something else I can get you?" Lenore hovered.

"No, thank you. These look good."

Lenore departed.

Pie watched her go. "Strange woman. I told her I'd rather she called me Pie instead of Dr. Lee and now she doesn't call me anything at all."

I laughed. "Lenore is an old-fashioned lady. She wants her boss to have all the trappings of a boss. I give her fits because she doesn't think a woman should be part of a management team. Don't give up on her too soon, you may be a civilizing influence."

"Your Aunt Bessie should only hear you say that. O.K. So let's get back to the main problem. If we get Delamain out of town, who's Acting Director when I'm not here?"

"After John, Frances Monk and Don have equal rank. Monk is out of the question -- for reasons that I'd like to talk to you about."

"Will Cromarty get in the way of the investigation?"

"No. His nose won't even be out of joint. Don doesn't have chain-of-command hang-ups."

"O.K., tell Lenore. So what's with Monk? Is she that skinny woman with the office off the reception room?"

"That's Monk." I told Pie about Monk's problem and the solution we had cooked up.

"Do you think the Department will play along?"

"Yes. Particularly if you hint that she might do something embarrassing if she stays around."

Pie made a note. "O.K."

"If she leaves, you'll have an SES slot to play with -- if we keep enough budget to pay salaries. You may want to bring in someone senior to honcho the biotech side."

"I can do that myself. I think I got too many chiefs now. Why do I need such a big staff?"

"You don't. You need someone to be Acting Director when you're not around and someone who isn't John to go to policy-level meetings when you're busy or don't want to go. If you can foist John on some other agency you won't need that SES slot. They have to be SES for political reasons. You need an Exec Officer, unless you want to count paper clips. And you need someone to do the high-level junk work -- although that recommendation may reflect my desire to keep my job. Other than that, I think you can rely on the senior tech staff.

Don can tell you who's competent and who's not. The SES slot will come in handy if you need an extra inducement to bring in a senior technical person you want. As you may have gathered from my title, what people do doesn't necessarily match what they're called."

"What do you do here, Bea? If you're an economist, I'm a hootchy-kootcher."

"I do the high level junk. One of the things about Government is that it generates a tremendous amount of junk. For instance, do you know how the budget process works?"

"I can tell by your face that it doesn't work the way I think it works. O.K., how?"

"Don and Stevie will give you most of the details. To understand what I do all you really have to know is that during the budget process at least seven different units have the right to get into your knickers -- the budget guys over at DoTI, then the management guys at DoTI, after them OMB, the staffers on the Authorization committee in both Houses of Congress, and finally the staffers on the Appropriations committees. None of them are technical, all of them have the right to ask questions and get a 24-hour turnaround on the answers, and any one of them can wreak havoc with your budget. You need someone who can translate what we do into something those guys understand. You could use a smart techie, like Alex, but then he'd never get his real work done."

"Why doesn't the Director do most of it? It sounds important enough."

"The same reason you can't use a techie. You have better things to do with your time. Which isn't to say you don't have to get involved. The budget will get a phantom cut at two places before it gets to the Hill -- at DoTI and at OMB. You'll have to go over and appeal. That part of the process is called the 'reclama'."

"So why don't we explain the program right the first time and avoid the phantom cuts?"

"Because the first time we send it over, we have to explain the whole program in a hundred words or less. Like an essay contest. You might be able to justify the purchase of a photocopier in a hundred words, but I haven't been able to figure out how to do it for a program that includes four biotech, five computer, and two telecommunications projects. Not to mention our main mission of looking at exports."

"*Vey is mir*. So what happens if we don't get through OMB with a budget we can live with?"

"We do what we're doing now. If you lose in OMB you can take your case to the Hill. That's O.K. as long as you don't get caught -- unless they're Washington Monumenting. Then they won't catch you on purpose."

"That's nutsy! Why are we talking about this now anyway?"

"Because you asked what I do here. I'm the one who responds to the idiot questions. There's a similar, but somewhat truncated process with the Office of Personnel Management over personnel slot allocations. Among other junk. Either you have a designated junk-dealer, or you have to get help from the techies -- who not only are too busy doing what they were hired for, they aren't very good at slinging crap, anyway."

"O.K., O.K., I won't fire you. That's enough for now. We'll have to talk some more -- particularly about what I should do on the Hill -- but I've had enough *mishegass* for one morning. I wanna talk to you some more about Stafford's murder. Do the cops really think it was an accident?"

"Apparently. That's what the officer said when he told us to go home on Friday. They spent a little while talking to Alex right after it happened, but that seems to be the extent of their activity."

Pie looked at his watch and winced.

"Where are you staying tonight, Pie?"

"I'll get a hotel."

"Why don't you come home with me?"

Uncharacteristically, Pie squirmed. "Ah, you and Alex, ah, you won't be embarrassed? I mean, ah..."

"Pie! We're all grown-ups."

Pie chuckled. "You got a deal. I'd like to talk to the two of you about what happened on the roof."

At 5:00 I went down to Alex's lab. He was there, staring glumly at his microcomputer. "No flashes of inspiration?"

"No. I've been freezing my heinie off on that damn roof all day seeing if I could winkle out a clue as to who did it, but if Tarzan knows, he ain't talkin'. Damn!"

"I invited Uncle Pie to spend the night at my house."

"Oh. Well, I guess I'll go home, then." Alex got up.

"He's expecting you to be there. I told him we were going to get married."

Uncharacteristically, Alex squirmed. "But Bea, won't, ah..."

"Alex, Pie wants to talk with you about Tarzan. If it'll make you feel better, you can sleep on the couch."

"Madam," said Alex, "that's going too far." He grabbed me and gave me a kiss. "When should we leave?"

"Well, at 5:15 Pie is supposed to find out from Lee Roy what Lee Roy's responsibilities are around here. That should take until 5:20, if Lee Roy spins it out."

Alex laughed, then sobered. "I've been going around in circles all day. What's so bad about this is that we've finally got someone at the head of this place who can pull it all together. But even with a guy like Pie here, I'm not sure we can survive if I don't figure out whodunit. I feel like I'm letting the guy down. Not to mention you and everyone else who works here."

I kissed him. "Maybe you'll think of something if we talk it through tonight. Two fresh minds might inspire you."

"Hope springs eternal. Let's go up to your office and wait for Pie."

At 5:30 Lee Roy walked past my office, on his way from his encounter with Pie. Alex grinned at me. "He must really have padded his job description."

Pie came in a few minutes later. "Where'd that lout come from? Do you know what he said to me?"

"What?"

"He said, 'The problem is that those technical jaspers expect us to do their work for 'em.'" The imitation was wickedly accurate. "'Now there's no reason in the whole wide world why they cain't do their own writin' and figger out their own budget and all that. They expect the Director's staff to wipe their asses for 'em.' What does that *schmuck* think LIT's here for?

"Don't answer, I can guess. You know, he actually offered to act as my Deputy. 'To 'he'p me run the place'. Can I fire him?"

"I could give you a tutorial on RIFs and bumps, but the short answer is no, not right away. The best you can do is give him a real job and then try to fire him for cause when he doesn't perform. But that'll eat up weeks of your time and the process is so elongated that it'll take him past his normal retirement date before it's finished."

"Nuts! O.K. But I want some of the offices moved anyway. I want to be closer to where the work gets done. And I want you and Don near the technical area too. Get the offices reassigned, Bea, and put that bucket of slime somewhere out of my sight."

Pie lowered one of his elegant buttocks onto the corner of my desk. "How far have you gotten, Alex?"

"This morning, I finally figured out how it might have been done." Alex gave Pie a quick recap of the hypothesized method. Pie, despite his claim of being a technical lox, had no trouble following the narrative.

"So someone could have copied the code from your hard disk, tampered with it, recompiled it, and loaded it onto the micro before the demonstration?"

"Theoretically. After I left the meeting this morning, I tested it."

"And?"

"It would work."

"How did someone get to your machine?"

"No problem. We don't do much classified work here, and the secure work we *do* do is kept together under lock and key. Security is lax in the rest of the place. The Departmental guards at the door stop anyone who tries to leave carrying a hunk of equipment, but other than that, we're pretty loose. I don't often lock my lab door during the working day and anyone could wander in when I'm not there -- during lunch, for instance."

"And no one would notice?"

"No. There are lots of people who could legitimately be in my lab. My technicians, for instance. Delamain. Don. Bea comes down. Steve Chandler and Dubble come in for briefings once in a while. Even that funny guy that works for you, Bea."

"Ben?"

"Yeah. Since we started planning the demo, almost everyone on the Director's staff sticks their head in once in a while to see how we're coming along."

"So about how long would it take to copy the program onto a floppy?"

"Not long. Less than five minutes."

Pie scratched his chin. "So let's take five minutes and time it."

We walked down toward Alex's lab. Most of the offices were filled with engineers still beavering away. "Your guys work late," Pie remarked.

Alex nodded. "It's interesting work."

We entered Alex's lab and Pie rapped on the micro. "Is this the assassin? Never know it to look at him."

"It's his twin brother. The real culprit is still on the roof. Should I start timing it?"

Pie shook his head. "Go out in the hall and come in again. Bea and I'll start timing as soon as you open the door."

Alex walked out. Pie laid his watch on the desk where he could see it easily. I have a gadget watch with a timer. I punched the button as Alex re-entered the lab.

He walked over to the micro and turned it on. While it was booting he took a floppy out of the disk file and put it into the drive. He typed the instruction to copy Tarzan, waited for the copy, took the floppy out, turned off the machine, and walked out of the lab. I punched the button to stop the timer.

Alex came back in. "How long?"

Pie was strapping his watch back on. "I got a minute four seconds. What'd you get, Bea?

"A minute three."

Pie grinned. "Close enough for government work. Where do you want to go to eat?"

"Why don't we eat at my place? I'm not up to Aunt Bessie's standard, but I can manage something edible."

"Sold. Let's go."

We took Alex's car and headed for the bridge.

"Did you find anything, Alex?"

"Zilch. And I'm fresh out of ideas."

"Well, in the words of my remarkable wife, 'First eat. Then you can think.'"

"Pie," I asked, "Why are you coming to LIT?"

Pie looked out the window for a few minutes. "Toots, I'm near the end of a very rewarding career. With God's and Bessie's help, I took the potential I had and ran with it. But

I'm not sure that there's anyplace else in the world where a Jewish Chinaman would have been allowed to develop his potential the way I did. I owe this country something. So when the Secretary asked me if I'd take this job, I talked it over with Bessie and we decided that the invitation was a due bill and I oughtta pay it. It was a little awkward because I haven't been at MIT that long, but the dean was good about it. I think partly because he thinks I can get him some grants from here.

"I suppose you kids have noticed that modesty's not one of my obvious traits. I can help LIT. I can help LIT because the Secretary knows me and trusts me and because of that he'll give LIT the kind of backing that you haven't had before. And I can help LIT because I'm a terrific politician."

"You?" I blurted it out before I could stop myself.

Pie threw his head back and roared. "Believe it. I've got almost every honor a guy in my profession can get except the Nobel -- and it's too early to tell about that one. No one piles those things up without being a good, tough politician. We were talking about Frances Monk. Why do you think she never got the recognition she shoulda had? Because she's a woman? Uh uh. You better believe Bessie's a woman and look at the kind of recognition she's had. And if you think being a woman was a bigger handicap than being a Jewish

Chinaman, you got a screw loose. Naw. If you're a good enough, tough enough politician, the world'll salute. And Monk's no politician at all -- let alone a good one or a tough one.

"So where was I? Yeah. What does being a politician have to do with helping LIT? Well, if you're in Washington, kid, you're in politics. And if you're in politics you better be good at it." Pie settled back. "And I'm good at it."

Alex leaned over from his perch in the back seat. "How come Stafford was being replaced? Had he resigned?"

"That's what the Secretary told me and I suppose it's the literal truth. Whether he was asked to submit his resignation, I don't know. I think maybe. LIT's a technical outfit but the Director has to get out front in some of the international negotiations and a lot of people think Stafford's a clown. The Department took him to one negotiating session and then dropped him from the list. I dunno."

"He just got a $45,000 award," I remarked. "I wonder if it was a Golden Pay-Off. It wouldn't be the first time."

"I dunno," Pie repeated.

I pulled the car into the garage and we debarked.

In the kitchen, I asked, "How do lamb chops and potatoes grab you?"

Alex looked thoughtful. "Pie," he asked, "do you know how to make potato pancakes?"

"Do I know how to make *latkes*? Does a shad know how to roe?"

I made a mental note never to let Pie in the same room as Ben. Ever.

"Of course I know how to make *latkes*. You want to make *latkes*?"

"Yeah."

"O.K."

Alex looked at me. "Get out of the kitchen, she-creature, this is man's work."

And they shooed me out of my kitchen and proceeded to make *latkes*, interrupting my hour of relaxation only to ask me to find the (a) potatoes, (b) aprons, (c) salt, (d) food processor, (e) wooden spoons, (f) skillet, and (g) a cookbook with a recipe for *latkes*. Eventually, we ate the damned things and pretended they were digestible.

CHAPTER 13

March 13 (cont.) - 14, 1990

We cleared the *latke* remains from the table and settled down over coffee.

"O.K., so now we know that the guy had plenty of time to swipe Alex's program. When would it have been done?"

I did a quick calculation. "Last Thursday or Friday, I think. Alex was having trouble with the program before that and I don't think the bad guy would have taken a chance on copying a program with a serious glitch. If it got copied on the 6th or 7th, he would have had the week-end to change the program and de-bug it."

Alex concurred. "At the outside, it could have been done on the morning of the 9th, but that would have been cutting it close. And the lab was locked over the week-end, except when I was in it. A lot of the guys come in on Saturday and Sunday; he wouldn't have taken a chance on someone seeing him force the lock."

"O.K. Then what would he have to do?"

"Then he would have to wait until mid-morning of the 9th, when the mockup was in place. He'd have to go up the stairs to the roof, figure out the coordinates where Hump would be standing, turn on the micro, enter the coordinates onto his floppy, recompile his program and load it onto the hard disk, and remove his floppy from the micro."

"How much time would that take?"

"Well, the stuff we timed in the lab this afternoon only took a few minutes. So assuming that he knew the line in the program where the coordinates had to go, the whole thing on the roof should take less than five minutes."

"Would he know the line?" I asked.

"Unless he was a total moron. He had all week-end to identify it."

Pie considered. "So, to give himself a margin for error, the guy would figure he needed ten or fifteen minutes alone on the roof between the time the mockup was in place and the demo got started."

Alex and I nodded. "That would be roughly between 10:30 and 2:30."

Pie got up and poured himself another cup of coffee. "Anyone else want one?"

Both Alex and I held out our cups for refills, which emptied the coffeepot. "I'll put some more on," I said. "Keep talking."

"O.K." Pie thought for a while. "You sure it would only take five minutes?"

"Pretty sure. Maybe we should go back to LIT and time it."

We got our coats and went once more unto the breach. It was a humdinger of a night. Clear, with each star sharply delineated in the sky. Pie got out of the back seat and opened the door for me. "Can we leave the car on the street?"

"Yeh. Parking restrictions are lifted at night."

The March wind suddenly gusted and we ran for the building. We went through the night-hours signing in ceremony and pushed the elevator button. "Where should we start timing?" I asked. "Do we assume that the crucial time is all on the roof or should we start at the bottom of the stairs?"

"Stairs, I think," Pie answered.

We walked down the silent corridor toward the roof stairs. The offices were empty except for one cubicle where a lone Terminal Scientist was agonizing over his micro. When we got to the door Alex unlocked it and said, "Why don't you two go up before me? I'll time my climb up to the top door and then you start timing when I get to the roof."

Pie and I nodded and began our ascent. The maintenance crew had erected a protective tent over the equipment. The wind had picked up and the canvas was making flapping noises. Beneath the noise of the canvas

I could hear Alex's footsteps ringing on the metal staircase. I looked at my watch. After seven seconds, the door opened, Alex appeared, and I punched my timer.

Alex walked over to the hull, and located the spot where Hump had stood. He took a little calculator from his pocket and entered some numbers; examined the spot again, entered some more numbers and nodded. "I just figured the coordinates," he said.

He turned, walked to the micro, and turned it on. Took a disk from the small disk file on the computer tabletop, put it in the drive, and spent a few seconds poking keys and staring at the screen. He poked a few more keys. He looked up and grinned at us. "The coordinates are now entered on an imposter-Tarzan." He hit a key and waited for another few seconds. "We now have compiled the imposter." Another key, another few seconds. "It's been transferred to the hard disk."

Alex typed a few letters on the keyboard and Tarzan's arms began to move toward the glass jar; uncapped it; put it down; moved toward the stool. Alex hit the keyboard again as they reached the stool. The arms stopped. Alex got up, walked over to the table, and screwed the cap back on the jar. "We gotta assume that he tested his program and everything was in place when the demonstration started."

Alex picked up the arms, returned them to their original position, and turned off the micro. "How long?"

I punched the timer. "I get just a tad over seven minutes. What have you got, Pie?"

"Seven minutes on the head." He looked at Alex. "It coulda been done that way. You got no ideas how we can prove it, huh?"

"Not a one," said Alex.

We locked up, signed out, and drove home. "The coffee's reasonably fresh. Do we want a caffeine nightcap?"

We filled our cups and reassembled at the table.

"Alex," I asked, "what happens on the disk when someone runs a kamikaze program like that?"

Alex looked puzzled. "You want me to go through it again?"

"No, love. I understand how the thing functioned. But what happens inside the machine?"

"Ah. Remember, his program was encoded on the hard disk and the name of his program was automatically entered in the directory of that disk. When I typed 'Tarzan', his program was automatically copied from the hard disk to the random access memory."

"The RAM," Pie supplied.

"Then there were two identical programs, one on the hard disk and one in RAM?"

"That's right," Alex continued. "Then when the program was finished, the RAM copy was destroyed and the entry in the hard disk's directory was erased."

Absently, I stirred my coffee. "What happened to the version that was put on the hard disk?"

Pie and Alex looked at one another. "Unless," said Alex, "he managed to put another program in the same place -- that is, wrote over it..."

"It should still be there," Pie finished.

"Hot damn," I said, "then all we have to do is find it."

"Bea," said Pie, "without the directory, I'm not sure it can be found."

"Sure it can," Alex said. "We can use one of the Norton Utilities. Un-erase should turn it up."

"Are you kidding us?" Pie asked.

"No, no. The Norton Utilities have been around for years. It might take hours to search the hard disk, but I can do it."

Pie shrugged. "If you say so."

"There's a problem though, Pie. If someone knew enough to rewrite my Ada program, he sure as hell would know how to get rid of the evidence."

"Not necessarily." I fetched the coffeepot and poured. "We've been sending Director's staff members to a course on Ada and they don't know much else."

"You've been doing what?" Pie asked.

"I can explain it, Pie, if you want to take the time now."

Pie shook his head. "For now, I'll take your word for it. *Oy*, what a place! Listen, I gotta go to Boston in the morning. Let's make a few assumptions and you two test them while I'm gone. Let me know if they prove out. If not, I'll be back Wednesday and we can try something else. You got something to write on, Bea?"

I found a pen and paper. "What are the assumptions?"

"First," Pie said, "it was someone who could reasonably be in Alex's lab without looking out of place."

"That doesn't eliminate a whole lot of people," Alex remarked.

"Outsiders," said Pie.

I shook my head. "Not even all of those. Someone like Mauve -- Hump's wife -- might have come in late in the day and stayed until after the main entrances were closed. That way, she wouldn't have to show identification and sign in. All she would have to do is wait until Alex left and then walk into the lab. She would have to sign out, of course, when she left, but that wouldn't cause any insuperable problems."

Alex was skeptical. "That's unlikely, Bea. I lock my office when I leave for the day."

Pie asked, "Could someone get into the lab without a key?"

I nodded. "Yeah. These aren't dead bolts. I use my credit card to push back the locking mechanism when I lock myself out of my office."

Alex was still unconvinced. "That would be awfully conspicuous. It's one thing for someone to walk into an open office. But to stand out in the hall jimmying the lock is something else. And we're looking for someone who would be inconspicuous."

"That person would only be conspicuous for a minute or two. Besides, the bad guy could have waited until the place was clear. There was only one person working on your wing tonight."

"O.K.," Pie said. "We can consider outsiders for purposes of the list, but check out the more likely stuff first. We can move on to the others if we draw blanks. What's the next assumption?"

"I think we can assume that this wasn't someone's idea of a practical joke," Alex said. "Whoever did it had some reason to want Hump dead."

"Let's talk about that for a minute," Pie said.

"C'mon, Pie," I said, "no one would do something like that as a joke."

"Not unless they were completely *mishugeh.* But there could be reasons that weren't personal. Like someone wanting to sabotage the robotics program."

"Is that a credible motive?" Alex asked.

"Yeah. It's a credible motive, but I don't see it being done this way. This was a pretty spectacular murder, but it's gonna be a two-day wonder in the press and it won't put the program on hold. The most it'll do is stop these crazy demonstrations before we've got something solid to show. Whose nutsy idea was this circus anyway?"

I scrutinized the ceiling and silently prayed that this was a rhetorical question. It was.

Pie continued, "I don't think it will even cause Congressional hearings. But there could be some other non-personal motives. Was Stafford mixed up in any secret stuff?"

I nodded. "He had all the clearances. But since I've only got limited clearance I've no way of knowing whether anything was going on now. He did mention that there was some classified reason for not exporting one of the telecommunications do-hickeys."

Pie grunted. "That's a wasp's nest. Tell you what we better do. Let's concentrate on the private motives for now. If it turns out that we can put together a good case for it being an impersonal murder, I'll talk to the Secretary and ask him to call in the Fibbies or the Spooks. He's overseas right now so that'll have to wait until next week. For now, let's go with the assumption that someone wanted Stafford dead, get as much information as we safely can, and -- unless we turn up a national security angle – take the case to the local cops. No matter who we call in, I'll talk to the Secretary first."

"What if," asked Alex, "we turn up some convincing evidence one way or another and the Secretary tells you to keep your mouth shut?"

"First of all," Pie answered, "I know the guy and he won't do that. But if he should all of a sudden turn into someone else -- someone who wants to hush up a murder -- I'll leave this job before I get here and take the murder public myself. Is that the answer you wanted to hear?"

"It is that." Alex grinned.

"O.K., then. Let's get on with it. What about the other half of the opportunity question?" Pie looked at Alex. "Your re-enactment showed the murderer figuring out the coordinates and entering them into his program after the mock-up was in place, right?"

"You got it," Alex said. "He'd have to be alone on the roof sometime between 10:30, when the DoTI graphic's crew finished, and 2:30 when the demo started."

"Could he have done it any other way?"

Alex shrugged. "None that I've thought of so far."

"Let's leave access to the roof as an assumption." I scribbled on my pad. "Anything else?"

"I think it's a safe assumption that the murderer knows Ada," Alex said.

"That may be the only safe assumption," I muttered. I wrote it down.

"How about not knowing enough about programming to erase the 'kamikaze'?" Pie asked Alex.

"Very shaky assumption," Alex answered. "I'm not sure the bad guy had to be ignorant. He may not have wanted to take the extra time to do something that wasn't likely to be necessary. The longer he was up there the more likely he was to get caught."

Pie agreed. "You're right. Or he may have been interrupted and cut the process short."

I visualized the scene. "You can't take the elevator up to the roof. The only elevator that goes all the way up is the freight and the professional staff doesn't have access to it. So if someone interrupted him, that person would have had to climb the stairs, just as we did. How long did it take you to get up, Alex?"

"Ten seconds."

"I heard seven seconds of your climb and there wouldn't be any reason for the interrupter to go on tip-toe. It's possible that the killer heard someone and quit without erasing."

Pie thought about it. "Nu, good news and bad news. The good news is that there's a better chance that the program is still on the disk. The bad news is that we can't narrow the field as much as we thought we could. Let's leave the assumption in, but only on this first pass. Alex is right, it's shaky. What else are we assuming?"

None of us could think of any more assumptions, so I rewrote the paper legibly. Neatness counts. The paper, when I had finished, said:

Assumptions

1. Murderer is someone who could reasonably be in Alex's lab, alone, for at least a short time. (Probably correct)
2. Murderer is someone who had a personal reason to want Hump dead. (Possibly correct)
3. Murderer had time alone on the roof between 10:30 and 2:30 on Monday. (Probably correct)
4. Murderer knows how to program in Ada. (Almost certainly correct)
5. Murderer does not know enough about computers to erase his program from the hard disk. (Very shaky)

"O.K.," Pie said, "If we take those assumptions, who fits the bill? I don't know the cast of characters."

"Bea," said Alex, "you know the possibles better than I do. You'd better go through them."

"I'll draw a chart while you're talking," Pie offered.

"What's going to be on it?"

"Names of possibles first; whether they know Ada; whether they were in the building and had the opportunity to be in Alex's office and on the roof at the right times; what the motive could be; and whether they were technical lox enough to leave the program on the hard disk."

"Pie, we don't know most of those things for sure. I couldn't swear that someone had no chance to be on the roof alone. And motive is a wild-assed guess."

"I know. I'll structure the chart so that the safer assumptions come first and put question marks where we don't have information. You ever heard the term 'first order approximation'?"

"I've heard it. I'm not sure I know what it means."

Alex laughed. "It's what a scientist calls a wild-assed guess."

"Stop arguing, already, Bea. We've got to start somewhere."

I stopped arguing. "O.K., let's take Don. He certainly knows Ada, but as far as I know, the motive is weak. He was sore at Hump because he thought some of the things he was doing were against the best interests of the country -- and Don has some Draconian ideas about what should be done to traitors. But I can't see Don killing anyone."

"Neither can I," said Alex, "but we'd better list him as a possible."

"I guess. He was certainly in the building and he could reasonably be in Alex's office but I don't think he was on the roof alone. He'd know enough to erase the program."

"Good enough," Alex said. "Delamain next. Ambition as a motive. He was sure he would be the next Director."

Pie made a strangled noise.

"John was in the building and he was fiddling with the mockup at the right time. The guys were taking turns eating lunch, so I think they were all up there alone for at least a few minutes. There's no point in nailing that down now. If Unerase finds the program, we can check the opportunity more closely then -- or leave that to the cops. As far as Ada is concerned, he's the same as Don.

"Frances Monk is the other SESer, but I can't believe she's involved."

"Why not?" Pie asked. "From what you told me, she's got motive."

"You haven't talked with her. I don't think she's capable of programming any more. That requires some concentration and I just don't see her brain functioning the way it would have to."

"Does she know Ada?"

"I don't know. I don't know how long she's been pickled. If she was *compos mentis* in, say, '84 or '85, maybe."

"Keep her in, then."

"She was in the building. No reason to believe she was on the roof; she didn't come to the demo. And if she was capable of re-programming, she'd know enough to erase the disk."

Pie finished his Monk jotting. "Who else on the staff?"

"Lee Roy. I don't know if he actually thought he was in line for the Director's job..."

"What?" Pie was incredulous.

"The jerk kept saying he was going to get it. I can't imagine why he thought a GS15 had a shot at it, but he kept saying it. He may have just been putting us on."

"I don't know." Pie thought about it. "He had the *chutzpah,* if his interview with me is any indication. Keep going on Lee Roy."

"Ambition as a motive, then. He went up to the roof just before Delamain. He's in the Ada course -- but he claims he isn't bothering to learn the language. And he's certainly a technical lox."

"Why did Stafford keep that nerd around?"

"Beats the hell out of me," Alex answered.

"None of us have been able to figure it out, Pie. He seems to function as a sort of malevolent court jester. But I'm damned if I know why Hump would waste a slot on him."

"Weird." Pie stretched.

"More coffee?" Alex picked up the pot and poured three cups. "Does Chandler have a motive?"

"Not that I know of. He's been due for a promotion from 13 to 14 and Hump had a less-than-endearing habit of putting off signing those things until someone had a conniption. It was almost as if he were hoping that whoever was in for a promotion would do something wrong and then Hump wouldn't have to move the papers. But I think Stevie -- or anybody -- would have gone the conniption route before resorting to murder. Apart from that, he had the same opportunity and knowledge as Lee Roy. Except that Steve was making an effort to learn Ada."

Pie looked up. "Is that the whole staff?"

"No. I think you have to count Ben. He's not senior staff, officially, but he sure is around." I explained Ben and Pie wrote him in.

"Is that the lot of them?"

"Yeah, but there are three more we ought to add for the sake of completeness."

"Who?"

"Gus Schnabel, for one. Lenore saw him in the building that morning. He could conceivably have snuck into Alex's lab. Has anyone told you about Gus?"

Pie shook his head. I turned to Alex. "You take Gus, I'm getting hoarse."

Alex told Pie about Gus and Pie wrote.

"Who's next?"

"Freddy Langsteth, the OMB analyst that I mentioned."

"Why Freddy?" Alex asked. "We can't put the whole world on that chart."

"I haven't told you about her and Hump." I proceeded to do so.

"That Stafford was some guy," Pie remarked. "How come he survived as long as he did?"

I thought for a while. "It's a funny thing, Pie, but we liked him. Don and I only started to question our judgment when we found out about what he was doing to Gus. Hump always seemed like an amiable eccentric, who let us get on with our jobs. He was pleasant enough and he was amusing, sometimes unintentionally, but he never minded when we laughed at him. It's hard to dislike someone who keeps you amused."

"Bea," said Pie, "how can people as smart as you guys be so dumb? You said three more. Who's the other one?"

"Hump's wife, Mauve. Only for convention's sake, really. I suppose Hump had some insurance for her to inherit; he sure didn't have any other assets. He didn't even own the house he lived in. I suppose if we're speculating about Mauve, it's conceivable that she would murder Hump because of his womanizing. But so far as I know, she wasn't in the building, let alone on the roof."

"Would she know Ada?"

"Not unless she's a magnificent actress. She comes across as the quintessential dumb broad. Should we put Alex and me on the chart?"

"Are we making a work of art or a set of assumptions for you and Alex to test? Stop being a *shlmeil.*"

I was in the process of ceasing to be a *shlmeil* when the phone rang; I picked it up. It was Cal Tech calling for Pie. I handed him the phone. “Yeh, O.K., Yeh.” He hung up.

He was grinning. “The labs at Cal and at MIT are cooperating on some research, and things are going well. They want me to join a conference call. I think so that they can brag about how well they’re doing without me. Is it OK if I call in from here? I can put it on my credit card.”

I glared at him. “Sure. And I’ll charge you a buck and half for all the coffee you drank. Go make the call. You already know that I’m overpaid.”

"You're right. I forgot how much we're paying you. This might take a while. I'll use the phone upstairs. Meanwhile, you guys do the chart."

Off he went.

I started riffling through Pie's notes, Alex looking over my shoulder. Shortly, he got bored with that and began nuzzling my ear.

"Alex, cut it out!"

"O.K."

He began nuzzling my other ear.

Well, what's a poor girl to do? Cooperation is the basis of all human progress. We were happily cooperating when we heard Pie's footsteps on the stairs. Springing apart, we sat demurely on both ends of the sofa, which was where Pie found us.

"They had something to brag about," he began. Then looked at us suspiciously. He examined his notes, which were in exactly the stage he had left them. "Thirty-year-old adolescents," he muttered as he put a finishing flourish on his chart.

"O.K., kiddies, here's what we got."

Name	Ada?	Opportunity		Motive	Lox?
		Bldg.	Roof		
Don	Y	Y	N	Patriotism	N
John	Y	Y	N	Ambition	N
Monk	?	Y	N	Afraid of losing job	N
Lee Roy	Y?	Y	Y	Ambition	Y
Steve	Y	Y	Y	?	Y
Ben	Y	Y	Y	Afraid of losing job	Y
Gus	Y	Y	N	Vengeance, hope Case will be dropped	N
Freddie	?	N	N	Vengeance	?
Mauve	N	N	N	Inheritance? Jealousy?	?

"Well," said Alex, "now that we've got a chart, what do we do with it?"

Pie laughed. "Don't be a Philistine. This is chart for chart's sake. What's clear, is that if all of our assumptions are right and we have complete information, one of two guys could've done it -- Dubble and that Ben fella. If our assumptions are right and we're missing information on motive, Chandler joins the list. If our 'lox' assumption is wrong, then we can add Delamain. I think we should begin with the supposition that the assumptions are right. That means that we should concentrate on Dubble and Ben Whatsisname for starters. Dubble may claim he didn't learn Ada, but he took the same course as Chandler and Ben. Also, we should see whether we can find answers to the question marks. I don't want you guys to do too much. Don't go taking any risks; if it turns out that this has security or even industrial espionage connections, you could wind up in real trouble, God forbid. Bessie'd kill me."

"You're safe from Aunt Bessie's wrath. We don't even have a plan for beginning the investigation. Anyone want to finish the coffee?" I picked up the pot and Pie held his cup out.

"I'm an engineer," Alex said. "I don't know about murder investigations. I think that's part of the management science course. You got a glimmer of a plan, Bea?"

I put the coffeepot in the dishwasher. "Before we do anything else, we have to see if Un-erase can find the program. If it doesn't, we'll be back at square one."

"Well, let's assume Un-erase finds it. Then what?"

Nothing occurred to the management scientist. Or to the engineer or the biologist, either.

Pie got up. "I think we're all getting punchy. Why don't we sleep on it. We can talk about it again in the morning."

Despite the gallons of coffee, we all slept the sleep of the utterly exhausted.

Inspiration did not come with breakfast. Danishes, yes. Inspiration, no. We were still groping for a plan as we drove Pie to the airport.

"Pie," I said, "If Un-erase finds the program, I think Alex and I should talk to Don about a follow-up plan."

Pie looked at me. "You really trust that guy?"

"Absolutely."

"If I remember your words of last night, you liked Hump, too."

"That was different. I liked Hump because he was a pleasant man who didn't get in my hair. I didn't know him. I do know Don and I can't imagine him killing Hump that way."

Pie looked skeptical. "You gave us a motive, of a sort. Don't you think Cromarty could justify it as an act of patriotism?"

I shook my head. "It's not that. I have a hard time seeing Don as a killer, but if he ever did do something that horrendous, his motives would be 'moral'. He wouldn't choose a method that would put LIT in jeopardy. He believes that LIT is vital to the nation's well-being. In Don's view, using Tarzan to get rid of Hump could endanger LIT's existence. And that would literally be an act of sedition as far as Don's concerned."

Pie contemplated. "You agree, Alex?"

Alex agreed.

"O.K.", Pie said, "Bring Cromarty in on it -- but only if Un-erase finds the program."

We pulled up in front of the NYAIR terminal and Pie got out of the car. He leaned back to give me a kiss. "I'll see you Wednesday."

CHAPTER 14

March 14, 1990

Pie had taken the early plane out of National. So, despite driving him to the airport, Alex and I had time to take a leisurely drive to LIT. He gave me a little snoggle. "Please continue the enthralling story of your life. We had left the heroine, a newly made orphan, about to enter college. Did you inherit enough to take you through?"

I gave him a sour look. "I inherited enough to barely cover the funeral expenses. I picked up a scholarship that covered tuition and for the rest, I worked my way through."

"Doing what?"

"Waiting tables during a couple of terms. Worked in an office typing envelopes one summer. Sold ladies hats another summer."

"Ladies hats? You're kidding."

"Not at all. Selling ladies hats is an art form, the secret of which is that you tell all the big, fat ladies that the hat makes them look little and thin and you tell all the little scrawny ladies that the hat makes them look statuesque and well-rounded. Doesn't do to have a conscience. Eventually, I lucked out and got a job doing scut work for one of the University's vice presidents. And then on to grad school where I met Harry."

"What made you go into management science? Were the university administrators that good?"

"No, they were that bad. I was working for a funny little guy from Lebanon. I thought the world of him. Then something really rotten happened. A hidden camera was mounted in the lounge where the parking lot guys worked – you know, the guys who collect the money when people pull in."

"I know the guys – I paid them every day of my University life."

"Those guys. Anyway, the story that came out was that the camera caught them siphoning off some of the money. They all got fired."

"Well, they should have been fired."

"Sure, if that was the real reason. It wasn't. I found out the true story. They were suspected of being homosexuals and that's the act they got caught in."

Alex stared at me. "And they got fired for that? The administration hid a camera to prove that?"

"Yep. And my hero, the kindly vice president, was one of the instigating forces. Thus, I went into management science. I thought I could prevent that kind of stuff from happening, at least on my watch. That's one of the reasons I was so upset about what Hump did to Gus. Prevent it? I didn't even know about it!"

We arrived at LIT and parted at the fourth floor. Alex was going to check his messages and then hare up to the roof where he would put Un-erase through its paces.

"You think it will take hours, Alex?"

"It could. It depends on where the program is located on the disk -- if it's there at all. Un-erase just slogs through the disk sequentially. If the program is near the beginning of the sequence, I could find it in five minutes. There's no way of telling. I'll come down to your joint as soon as I find it."

I continued up to five and headed for my office. Stevie was in the corridor talking to Wilfred, the maintenance man. Wilf is a grotesquely fat, black man with a squeaky soprano voice. We all tried to engage him in conversation because he sounded so funny. Stevie broke off as I walked by. Awright," he said to Wilf, "I'll get a requisition, but it's such a little thing."

"No matter," squeaked Wilf, "no tickee, no laundry." He waddled off.

"What was that all about?"

"I want my door knob changed to one that has one of those lock things on the inside and Wilf wants me to file two tons of justification before he'll do the job. I thought that was gonna be the way it is, but I wanted to hear him say it."

I laughed. "Why do you want a lock on the inside?"

"I got that interconnecting door with Ben's office and he bounces in whenever he has something to say. I like Ben, but..."

"...he's a pain-in-the-ass," I finished.

I went into my office and began to deal with the accumulated crud. It was only a little after nine when I heard a very unmusical 'Modern Major General' approach. Could Alex have found the program? Alex could indeed have found the program. He scooted into my office, closed the door, and caught me in a bear hug. "Alex," I said, "would you find Wilf and ask him to put one of those lock things on my inside door knob?"

"Huh?" said Alex.

"I'll explain later. I think it's Don time."

We walked to Don's office. He was on the phone trying to draft a center fielder who didn't want to be drafted. "Sit. I'll be off in a minute." Don wound up the conversation.

"What's up?"

I trotted out the charts while Alex explained the situation. Don looked over my shoulder. "Do you really think I'd bump off that tub of lard out of a sense of patriotism?"

"If we thought so, we wouldn't be here."

"And what's this 'vengeance' thing after Freddie's name?"

That was not something I wanted to go into.

Alex came to my rescue. "Right now, we're stuck. We've got a pretty compelling argument for it being murder, not a screwy accident; and we've got a less convincing argument that it's one of two guys. The question is, where do we go from here?"

"Have you thought of the cops?"

"Yes," I said, "and rejected the thought. There's been a remarkable lack of police activity around here -- which almost certainly means that they haven't changed their minds about it being an accident. With what Alex found this morning, we could probably get them off the accident theory, but I don't see that they can do anything more than we can. Their computer people can't be nearly as good as you and Alex, and they don't know the staff. The only thing we get by going to the police, as far as I can see, is a lot of very unwelcome public speculation just in time for Pie's confirmation hearings. Pie is going to have a hard enough time without having to answer questions about which one of his staff is a killer. Besides, we're not sure which set of cops to call."

"Howzat?"

"Well," said Alex, "we don't know whether Stafford was killed because someone wanted to kill him or because of a situation. It's possible that the murder is related to national security or industrial espionage or something like that. In which case it's the FBI or the Spooks. We thought we ought to nose around just enough to build a good case for it being murder and to get some idea of whether it's a personal killing or a whaddyacallit -- an institutional murder, I guess."

Don leaned back in his chair and stretched his legs. "Yeah. Well, you guys have made good time so far. It won't hurt to take it one more step."

"You have put your finger on the problem, Mr. Cromarty," Alex said. "Just what the hell is the next step."

"Mmph. What would the bad guy have to do if he constructed a kamikaze?" Don mused. "He'd have to de-bug it, right?"

"Right."

"And if he had to de-bug it, he'd have to have more than one copy, right?"

"Right," said Alex.

"Why?", said I.

"Because the program blows itself up. What he probably did was make half-a-dozen or so copies and when one destroyed itself, he'd go to work on one of the spares."

"Aha."

"So the question is, are any of those spares lying around?"

We considered the question. Finally, Alex said, "It's a long shot, but so was finding the program on the hard disk."

"This is different, Alex," I said. "Anybody would know that the floppy should be erased by re-formatting. There isn't a hope in hell that we can find the spare."

Don wasn't listening. "If there's a spare, it's probably in Lee Roy's or Ben's office. Can we get rid of those guys for the afternoon, Bea?"

"Don, listen to me! The spares would have been destroyed."

"Bea," said Alex, "In the words of our leader, stop arguing, already. Can we get rid of Ben and Lee Roy this afternoon?"

"For heaven's sake. Yes. I can get rid of them. I'll find meetings for them to go to. I can send Ben and we can have Lenore tell Lee Roy that Pie told him to go."

"Good," Don said. "Better get to it now."

I scooted back to my office and looked at the meeting calendar. There was a lecture at the State Department for Lee Roy. Ben could be shipped off to one of the Urban Institute seminars on trade with the Third World. For all the good it would do us, that would get them out of the office for a good enough spell. I stopped at Lenore's desk and set it up.

"Have you had a chance to find out if Mauve wants us to sort out Hump's things?" I asked.

"I called her late yesterday and she wanted us to do it. I've already done the sorting, so you can take Mr. Stafford's things to Mauve whenever you have time." Lenore looked incredibly virtuous. "Perhaps you should look around the office and see if I've missed anything. Mr. Stafford's things are in the box on the coffee table." Not a single snorf. I rather missed the snorfs. Would Lenore one day explode from the pressure of hundreds of bottled up snorfs? I thanked her and went on my inspection tour.

Hump's box was unrevealing. Three umbrellas, fold-up variety. A folder of completed crosswords from the London Times. A photo of Mauve bulging out of a bikini. Another photo of a speck in the sky. I turned it over and read the inscription: Mauve Skydiving, 8/87 Several framed award citations and a florid certificate confirming that Hump was a bona fide member of the SES. Three floppy disks labeled, respectively, "International Congresses", "Biotechnology Worksheets", and "Export Policy." Why on earth had Lenore put them among Hump's personal things?

I trotted the floppies over to the micro and checked the contents. They were, respectively, "Galactic Gangsters", "The Ruins of Mu", and "Adventure". Didn't that banana ever do any work? I dropped two of the disks back in the box and wriggled Adventure into my pocket. If I was going to play detective, I'd have to talk to Lee Roy. And if I talked to Lee Roy, I'd need some excuse for seeking him out; presenting him with Adventure would serve. Gather ye conversation pieces while ye may. I finished rummaging in the box and moved on to the desk.

The in-box was overflowing with administrative junk, requests to serve on committees, invitations to functions long past, and interim reports on export analyses -- some of them dating back to January. At the bottom of the in-box was the set of documents (unsigned by Hump) supporting Stevie's promotion to GM14. Hump hadn't even begun to move the paper! I shifted Steve's documents to the top of the in-box and looked over at the out-box. Nothing there. Either Lenore had dispatched the dispatchable or else nothing much ever left Hump's office. Two sets of documents in the Pending folder. I picked them up, glanced at them, and sank down onto the desk chair.

What I had in my hands were two sets of documents (signed by Hump) supporting (a) Frances Monk's demotion from her Senior Executive Service position as Chief Scientist to a GS15 bench job and (b) Lee Roy's promotion to Monk's vacated slot. Lee Roy as Chief Scientist? What on earth could Hump have been thinking of? What made him think that OPM would certify a PhD-less GS15 Computer Specialist as Chief Scientist? And why would he go to all that trouble for Lee Roy when he hated so much as a page of administrative paper? I riffled through the documents to the top of the in-box and looked pages to the "Justification" section.

> While Mr. Dubble has not obtained a graduate degree [or an undergraduate degree, I thought] he has, during his long career with the Federal government, not only received graduate level training in the technologies central to LIT's

mission, but has demonstrated an unparalleled grasp of the scientific principles that underlie them [Lee Roy?] He has, on merit, risen to a position of eminence in the scientific world [Lee Roy Dubble?] as the attached material will attest...

I flipped to the testimonials. George Grot of DoTel had written a beaut. "Astounding knowledge of the intricacies..." From a Dr. Wassil Chernabronsky of Biofloton, "Scholarly comprehension of the field..." And from Dr. Nathan Rivington Forrest II of ADProformance, "Scintillating speaker with a grasp of both the fundamentals and the future..." [Our Lee Roy Dubble?]

I set Lee Roy's packet down and picked up Monk's. "Failure to stay abreast of the field...Dr. Monk's best interests to return to practical..." Not a word about drunk.

I started to return the documents to the Pending file, thought better of it, and put them in the top drawer of the desk. In her current phase of excessive zeal, Lenore might send them out without alerting Pie. Come to think of it, I'd better alert Pie.

I settled back in the chair and thought. Could Hump really pull something like that off? Monk: probably; Lee Roy: no way. Monk was in the SES where civil service protections were less rigid than for the lesser grades. Still, she might have made a fuss. Wouldn't help her case, but could queer Lee Roy's pitch if she were lucid enough to tell the truth. I opened the drawer and looked at the date lines on the documents. Undated. Hump must have been waiting for the results of the OPM audit on Monk. Certainly no mystery about how that would come out and if the audit report was attached to the papers, it would effectively quell any protest Frances might make. Thank God for small mercies. If Hump had kept his derriere in Washington, the OPM report most likely would have been completed and the papers moved. Pie could have stopped them, of course, but not without a lot of trouble and Pie didn't need a lot more trouble right now.

Hump really had been a crumb. Even if he had some legitimate, if arcane, reason for promoting Lee Roy to Chief Scientist [Chief Scientist?], he could have eased Monk out with an award. God knows he wasn't saving the Government money by doing it this way. Monk would have continued to draw her SES salary for three years -- a helluva lot more than any award she might get.

I kicked off my shoes, put my feet up on Hump's desk and continued to ponder.

However insensitive his method was, Hump undoubtedly could have freed Monk's slot. But getting Lee Roy into it? Uh uh. If it were only OPM to worry about, it might be possible. God only knows what OPM thinks are proper qualifications for a Chief Scientist. But that nomination would have to get through the Department -- layers and layers of Department. It wouldn't make it. Someone would want to see a scholarly publications list and Lee Roy didn't publish. Someone would want to see evidence that he had been an invited speaker at some scholarly convocation. Lee Roy didn't speak. And someone would want to see some academic sponsors -- not just three obscure bozos from middling companies. No way. Hump must have been dreaming if he thought he could get that through. Whatever the odds, though, Hump and Lee Roy must have thought they could bring it off. The master plan must have been for Lee Roy to wriggle into the SES, which would legitimize his candidacy for the Director's job when Hump left. Could he make a serious run at the job from that position? Only if Hump's departure was by choice. If that were the case, Hump would have some influence on the selection of his successor. Particularly if he could drum up some support from Industry. This was, after all, the

Department of Trade and Industry -- and Industry is the Department's constituency.

But what did this do to Lee Roy's motive for murder? Knocked it to hell, that's what. Even if Lee Roy had some other reason to obliterate Hump, he would certainly have waited for Hump to implement his part of the master plan. Phooey! Well, if it isn't Lee Roy, maybe we can pin it on Delamain. With Lee Roy out of the running, John was certainly my sentimental favorite.

The door opened and Lenore stuck her head in. "Do you need any..." Lenore stared at my feet. "Really, Bea!" Snorf. A lovely sound.

I swung my legs down and slipped my shoes on. "Lenore, what's Mauve's phone number?"

Lenore recited the number and I dialed. Mauve answered on the second ring.

"Mauve, this is Bea Goode. We have Hump's belongings packed up. When would it be convenient to bring them over?"

"Oh Bea, could you do it now? I'm just standing here in the middle of all of Hump's things and I don't know what to do and I'm so upset and I need someone to talk to. Could you come over now? I really need..."

"I can leave in about an hour, Mauve." I got the directions to Mauve's house, picked up Hump's box, and left his office. I was not looking forward to the visit with Mauve.

The other visit I was not looking forward to was with Lee Roy. Nonetheless, I knocked on his door.

"Awright."

I walked in. Lee Roy occupied a large, square office. The walls were lavishly decorated with photographs of Lee Roy and various dignitaries. At least Lee Roy claimed they were dignitaries. No one else had ever heard of any of them. Lee Roy himself was sitting behind a very large, very bare desk. He looked disconsolate but managed to give a fair-to-middling imitation of Lee Roy. "Well, if it ain't LuLuBelle her own self. Ya come to pour salt in the wounds?"

"Only if I you think you need more seasoning. I was packing up Hump's stuff, and I thought you might want this." I dropped the box on the floor and winkled the disk out of my pocket. "Here."

Lee Roy took the floppy and looked at it, puzzled. "Whaddo I want with the files on export policy?"

I laughed. "Don't judge a disk by its label. It's Hump's copy of Adventure."

"Well, damn. LuLuBelle, I am touched."

Oddly, I think that was the truth.

"Sit yourself down, woman. I oney got a minute. Your Chink wants me to go to a meetin' at State and I gotta run. You know anythin' about that?"

"No," I lied.

"Surprised me. From the little talk I had with him, I don't guess he likes me one little bit. Wouldna thought he'd send me anywheres in the civilized world. Shee-it, LuLuBelle. I thought I had it made. Now you didn' know it, but Hump had it set up for me to be Chief Scientist once we got ridda pore ole Monk. Papers are movin' through the system this very minute."

I must have registered some surprise because Lee Roy said, "Fact. Mrs. Dubble's little boy Lee Roy, Chief Scientist. Shee-it. I don't guess the Chink'll let that go through. You don't haveta answer that, LuLuBelle," he said kindly. "Winners and losers, honey, winners and losers. An' I think I jes lost this one." Lee Roy looked at his watch and got up. "I better haul my ass over to State. Lemme give you a piece of advice. You got a winnin' hand right now. Getcher enemies before they get you."

He stepped around Hump's belongings and out the door.

He poked his head back in as I was picking up the box. "But jes so there's no confusion, LuLuBelle, ole Lee Roy ain't your enemy."

When I got back to Don and Alex, those two noodles were plotting just as if they had a sure thing.

"Here's what we're gonna do, Bea." Don had assumed a general's stance. "As soon as Dubble and Goldfarb are out of here, we're going to get into their offices and make copies of all their floppies."

Alex interrupted. "What if they lock their doors? If we try to jimmy them, someone sure as hell will catch us."

"Not a problem," I said. "I just saw Lee Roy off and he left his door open. Lenore has duplicate keys, anyway. If Ben's door is locked, Don can tell her that Pie called asking for Ben's information on trade statistics and he needs the keys to get into his office to look for them.

"Once you have copies of all the floppies, then what?"

"We split them up and take them home. I don't think we should do this in the office. Both Ben and Lee Roy have an awful lot of disks, Don. Maybe a hundred apiece."

"Yeah. That's why we'll split them up. As soon as one of us finds something, we call the others."

I was still dubious. "The only thing I've used my micro for is word processing. I've never manipulated a disk with a program on it -- let alone an Ada program. I'm not sure I won't mess up my portion."

"You may have a point, Bea," Alex agreed. "I think it will save time if you take the unlabeled disks and examine them to see if there's anything on them. If you find something, call Don or me and we can do the inspection."

"Their new disks!" Don smacked his head. "We almost forgot about them. The program could have been put on an unlabeled disk and hidden in the box with their unused ones. We'd better take their new disks and replace them. I'll pick up some boxes in the storeroom."

"While you guys are burgling and copying disks, I'm going to run Hump's stuff over to Mauve. Maybe I can fill in some of our question marks while I'm there."

"Good hunting," said Don.

"Be careful," said Alex.

I saluted and left.

CHAPTER 15

March 14 (cont.) - 16

Hump and Mauve rented a ramshackle little house at the Georgetown end of Foxhall Road -- just before Foxhall is transformed from being expensive to being outlandishly expensive. I thought about taking my car. Then I thought about trying to find parking space when I returned. And then I hailed a cab. Washington's cabbies are divided into three types -- Old Washingtonian White and Talkative, Old Washingtonian Black and Born-Again, and Middle Eastern and Incomprehensible. I drew Type 1 for this trip.

"You work there?" He pointed his head at the LIT building.

"Yep."

He cut off a hinged tour bus. Tires squealed. "SoB's think they own the streets. D'ja hear about the guy that went off the roof? Right on Independence Avenue, would you believe? Just about where I picked you up." He cut off a municipal bus. More squealing tires. "SoB's think they own the streets. I was right across the street when this guy comes sailing down. Splat. Put you off your feed for a week."

He turned around. "D'jou know him?"

"Yep."

"Unnerstand a robot gave him the shove. Just like that. Splat." He cut off an out-of-town tourist bus. Tires again. "SoB's think they own the streets. Makes you think, donnit. Imagine a robot doing a thing like that. Just goes to show."

He cut deftly into the right lane, whipped around another taxi, scooted back into the left lane and came to a sudden stop at the red light.

The cab behind us screeched to a halt and the driver jumped out and stuck his head in our left front window. Black and Born-Again. "You SoB, you think you own the street?" Brothers under the skin.

"Up yours," my cabbie rejoined.

The light changed and the Black guy ran back to his cab. My cabbie said "Splat" again. "Wonder what the hell that robot thought he was doing. You gotta watch those things. They're like kids. Got minds of their own and they won't listen to nobody. You got kids?"

"No."

"Well, count your stars. I got kids. Five of 'em. They're like that robot. Turn your back for a minute and -- splat." He pulled up in front of Mauve's house. I paid him and lugged the box up the front steps, to the rhythm of the schnauzer yapping. Mauve opened the door before I had a chance to ring. The little schnauzer trotted out and down the steps.

"Brute, come back here!" Mauve called.

The schnauzer trotted back.

"Does she always come back when you call?" I asked.

"Oh yes," Mauve said, leading me into the house. "She's wonderfully well-trained. Hump used to spend hours every morning training her."

Mauve was, as usual, heavily cosmetiqued. Mascara, eyeshadow, liquid tan -- the works. She was encased -- barely -- by a black leotard. I wondered if this was her version of mourning garb. She stopped suddenly in the middle of the living room and wailed, "Oh Bea, who's going to do all those things for me now?" She threw her arms around me and I dropped the box on my foot.

Mauve picked up the scattered papers and crammed them back in the box while I hopped around shaking my leg. The schnauzer dashed frantically back and forth between us. Finally, Mauve and I sat down and regarded one another across the cluttered coffee table.

The little room had the aura of a bundle waiting for the Goodwill truck. It contained the two upholstered chairs which currently held Mauve and me. They were roomy, comfortable, and the stuffing was coming out. In one corner was a delicate-looking chair which, to my untutored eye, looked like a for-real Queen Anne. It was covered with schnauzer-claw scratches. Spilling out of the brick-and-board book cases and onto the floor were stacks of paperbacks -- mostly Gothics -- indiscriminately mingling with computer-book-club offerings and pop-philosophy tomes. Skis, rackets and scuba gear were stacked against a wall. I looked around for relics of Mauve's skydiving career, but none were in evidence.

"Bea," Mauve said, "what am I going to do? We had everything arranged just perfectly and now it's all apart again. I mean, we were going to Denver -- I even joined a ski club and a country club and bought a house and most of the furniture. And we were looking for another little house in the mountains, you know, so we could get away from the pressure and everything and now I just don't know. I just don't know anything." She fished a Kleenex from the box on the table and daubed at an eye. Carefully.

"You'll recover," I said gently. "It takes a while, but you'll recover and find your life again."

"No, no," she said. "I mean, I know you're a widow, too, but you're different. You don't care about things like I do. You don't need anyone. I want all those things and now I may never get them. You just can't know how I feel."

Which pretty much took care of my incipient empathy. "I guess you're right, Mauve," I said. And metaphorically crossing my fingers, "When was Hump going to join DoTel?"

"Oh," said Mauve, "he's already on the payroll. It would be much worse for me if he weren't. I mean, this way, I get his insurance from both places and some other benefits and things. It's nice of you to worry about me, Bea, but money-wise, I'm o.k. I mean, the lawyer said I was o.k. as long as I didn't spend it all at once and he thinks he should set something up -- a trust or something. But it's not like now, with Hump having two salaries for almost a year and being able to buy almost anything and go on lots of trips."

Untypically, I was speechless. Didn't that pea-brain understand what she was saying? She prattled on.

"But I wanted to move to Denver and now I can't."

"Why not, Mauve? It won't be the same without Hump, but Denver is still there."

"Oh, Bea, you just won't understand. Hump was going to be real high up in the company and I'd have lots of things to do and people to do them with because people always hang around people who are high up. People won't hang around me anywhere now. And I won't have anyone to do things with anymore." Tears and mascara were trickling down Mauve's cheeks.

"Don't you have family?"

"Well, there's Mavis -- she's my sister -- but I'm not speaking with her anymore. Not since Lee Roy tried to do what he did."

I was starting to feel dizzy. "What does Lee Roy have to do with not speaking to your sister?"

"Well, she's his wife, isn't she?"

So now I knew why Hump kept Lee Roy around.

Mauve went on, "And he tried to get Hump's job at DoTel and Elaine, that's George's wife, told me and I told Hump and Hump said he was going to fix Lee Roy's clock but not to tell Lee Roy we knew, so I'm not talking to Mavis."

"Mauve, hold it a minute. Start at the beginning."

"All the way at the beginning? Well." Mauve settled herself and the schnauzer jumped on her lap. "Lee Roy and Mavis got married when Lee Roy was still at that other Department a long time ago."

I hadn't really meant that far back, but there was small hope of stopping Mauve in full flight.

"Anyway, Lee Roy knew Hump for a long time because Lee Roy used to come out to the west coast on trips and when he was there he used to play in this poker game that Hump used to play in. Anyway, Hump was getting a divorce and Lee Roy and Mavis thought he'd be a pretty good catch for me so the next time Lee Roy went to the coast, Mavis and I went with him and he introduced me to Hump. Hump was going with some awful fat lady then but Lee Roy said she didn't matter."

So much for Freddie.

"Anyway," Mauve continued, "Lee Roy was sort of right, because Hump would have been a pretty good catch except we didn't know he'd have to pay all that alimony and child support. That bitch he was married to really took him. And now when we finally got enough money to do what I wanted, it's all ruined again!" Mavis wiped her eyes in earnest.

"But what was it that Lee Roy did that made you stop talking to your sister?"

"Oh, when it started to look like Hump's new job was going to be real good, Lee Roy talked to George and tried to talk him into giving him, you know, giving Lee Roy the job instead of Hump. As if they would! But you know Lee Roy."

Unfortunately, I did. "What did Hump do?"

"He fixed his clock."

"How?"

"Well, I don't know, do I? I mean Hump was afraid if he told me then I'd tell Mavis so he didn't tell me. I stopped speaking to Mavis because I thought if I wasn't speaking to Mavis Hump would know that I wouldn't tell her. But he didn't tell me anyway."

I was getting positively fascinated with the Stafford/Dubble family affairs. "But what did you tell Mavis when you stopped speaking to her?"

Mauve looked at me blankly. "Well, if I wasn't speaking to her I couldn't tell her anything, could I? Would you like some coffee, Bea?"

"Yes, thank you. While you're making it, perhaps I can look through Hump's desk to see if there are any papers here that should be brought back to the office."

"Oh. O.K. His stuff is in there. You want me to show you where things are?"

"Let me take a look. I'll holler if I need help."

Mavis went off to the kitchen, followed by schnauzer. "In there" was through a door just to the right of the scuba gear. Hump's study was nearly twice as large as the living room, but decorated in the same style. Papers randomly strewn. Books abandoned. Poker chips hither and yon. On the corner of the desk a sere banana peel. I felt a swelling of admiration for Lenore; maintaining a semblance of order in Hump's office must have been an heroic endeavor. One corner of the room was occupied by a micro, topped by a shaky stack of disks. The micro had a DoTI property tag affixed. I turned the machine on and fed it the disks, one by one. What I learned was that Hump had an absolutely amazing collection of computer games.

A longish refectory table served as a desk. I walked over to it and began pawing through the papers. Bills. Utility bills and dentist's bills. Overdue rent bills and credit card bills. Book club bills. Garage bills. Hotel bills. If someone sold it, Hump had bought it on credit. I wondered if Mauve would have anything left from Hump's collection of life insurance policies and pensions. I finally found the DoTel folder on the far left corner of the table. It contained Hump's employment agreement, dated June 15, 1989. That crooked hunk of blubber! Hump's conditions of employment were separated into two phases. For the first year, his duties were unspecified and his title was "Senior Planning Advisor." On June 15, 1990 he was to become Director of Corporate Development reporting to the Vice President for Planning and Marketing. The agreement had the normal provisions for moving expenses, bonuses and stock options. It was signed by Vice President for Planning and Marketing, George Grot. No wonder Grot behaved as if he owned Hump. He did own Hump.

The folder also contained some DoTel annual reports (they were doing nicely), employee benefit information (standard), and a printed document, marked in red, describing the business and assets of HiTeKor, a company to be formed from the merger of Do-Tel, Biofloton, and ADProformance. The document was dated March 8, 1990. Hoo, Momma.

Mauve came in just as I was slipping the papers back in their folder. "Did you find anything, Bea?"

"Just the microcomputer. If you don't mind, I won't try to lug it back now. I'll have someone with more muscles come get it."

"O.K. I didn't want it anyway; I can't type. The coffee's ready. It's lunchtime but I don't have anything in the fridge, so I guess it's just coffee and Oreos. I'm not much of a hostess, just now."

We went back into the living room and sat down. Mauve had cleared some of the clutter off the table. She had also re-made her face.

"If you'll give me a list, I'll stop after work and do your shopping for you. You shouldn't skip meals."

Mauve gave the schnauzer a cookie. "That's nice of you but I was going to go out anyway. I'm pretty sick of hanging around this dump. Anyway, I haven't been missing meals. I just ate everything up."

And with that, we parted, the dog yapping a fond farewell. I walked toward Georgetown, gesticulating madly every once in a while until a cab stopped. A Type 3 driver.

"Vere?"

"The DoTI building."

"Vadgia?"

"On Independence Avenue."

"Hah vadgia?"

"By the Smithsonian castle."

"Hoo vadgia?"

A flash of inspiration. "Just across from the Sackler Gallery. You know, where they have all the Islamic art."

"Hah!" We sped off and I leaned back to think. My morning of detecting had certainly been fruitful but what could Mauve have been thinking when she told me all that? Not even Mauve could be that dumb. Hump and Lee Roy -- a really great pair of guys. At which point I realized that not even Mauve was that dumb; just righteously vindictive.

Nothing was going to happen to Mauve because of the revelations. Even if DoTI could legally recover some of Hump's ill-gotten gains, in this scandal-shy town, they wouldn't. But in the event that Hump hadn't had time to "fix Lee Roy's clock", telling me about his perfidy surely would. Mauve certainly must know that Lee Roy is not my favorite colleague. Even if she thought I would condone a blatant effort to arrange a spot of conflict-of-interest profiteering in general, I wouldn't condone it by Lee Roy. I'd tell someone and get his clock fixed. Exactly what was going to happen. Good thinking, Mauve.

The cab drew up to the curb and I hopped out. Don and Alex had just come back from lunch and were among the crowd waiting for the elevator. We got on together. "How'd you do?" I whispered.

"O.K." Alex whispered back. "One down. We're waiting for the other guy to leave." And aloud, "Let's stop in my lab, it's easier to talk there without being interrupted."

I shook my head. "I think we'd better call Pie. Let's commandeer the little conference room and use the conference phone."

We got off at five. "Did you get that much, Bea?"

Did I ever."

Don stopped at Lenore's desk while Alex and I scooted into the conference room. Don followed almost immediately. "I told Lenore to locate Pie and connect him here. What's up?"

"Let's wait for Pie -- it's too long a story to go through twice."

Pie, apparently, was easily locatable because the call came through in a few minutes. "*Nu*?"

I went through the whole thing, beginning with the discovery of Stevie's, Monk's and Lee Roy's personnel folders.

"Sheesh," Alex said. "I must be naive, but I'm shocked."

"You should be," Pie said, grimly. "Stafford's beyond punishment, but I'm gonna have Dubble's *tuchas*."

"Good luck," Don said, "but I don't think that trying to get another job is a crime."

"No, but knowing about Stafford and not reporting it is. At least I think it is. We'll see. I'll tell you one thing; Do-Tel's in trouble. Alright, already, lemme see if I got this straight. One: Stafford hadn't moved Chandler's promotion. Two: papers to demote Monk were in the pending file. Three: papers to make Dubble the Chief Scientist, God forbid, were also in the pending file," Pie had evidently taken notes.

"Four: Stafford has been on DoTel's payroll since last June. Five: Dubble tried to euchre Stafford out of his job. Six: Stafford knew about Dubble's game, didn't tell Dubble he knew, but was going to do something bad to him. And Seven: there's a red herring on DoTel."

"What do you mean a red herring?" I yelped. "That's an honest-to-God clue if I ever saw one."

Pie and Don laughed. Don said, "Bea, a 'red herring' is the trade term for a proposed prospectus to the SEC. It means that the new company they were forming was going to be a public corporation."

"They were asking the SEC's permission to sell stock," Pie added.

"Oh," I said.

Alex squeezed my hand and whispered, "I didn't know that either." And aloud. "Why don't we take this point by point and see what we can make of it?"

"Sold," Pie agreed. "The first one is Chandler's promotion."

"Nuthin'," Don said. "All it does is confirm a weak motive. It doesn't make the motive any stronger."

"Same with the next point," I said. "It confirms Monk's motive."

"I think it does more than that," Alex objected. "It's one thing to suspect that Hump wouldn't stop OPM from demoting her; it's something else to know that Hump was taking an active part. If she knew about those papers, that is."

Don and I nodded. "Yeah," Pie said. "She would probably figure he sicced OPM on her in the first place. And she'd probably have been right. The next one is Dubble's promotion. Could Hump have got that through?"

"Not likely. I've been thinking about that. I don't think Hump wanted to get it through. I think that's how he was going to 'fix his clock'. Lee Roy would never have made it to the Chief Scientist slot, but Hump could have created a different SES job for him once Frances' slot was available. Deputy Director or Director of International Affairs. Something that doesn't require scientific credentials. If the object was to give Lee Roy a shot at being Director of LIT, the Chief Scientist's job isn't a particularly good position to shoot from. And once Lee Roy was rejected as Chief Scientist, DoTI would be very reluctant to put him into another SES job right away. It would look too much like favoring a buddy. I think Hump was setting him up."

"Damn right," Don said. "What a pair of sleazes!"

"Next point," Pie continued. "Stafford's been on DoTel's payroll for almost a year. We already talked about that."

"Except that it means he resigned, rather than getting canned," I said.

"Not necessarily, he may have seen a canning coming before he put his resignation in. He probably intended six months notice. Those sleazes!" The more he thought about it, the more upset Don became.

"I don't see that it makes much difference," Alex said, "except that it would be more satisfying if he had been canned."

"Alright, we can take five and six together. The shenanigans with the job and Dubble's clock."

"Mauve said that Lee Roy tried for the job after the job started looking good. That must have been when he found out about the mergers and stock offerings. There were stock options in Hump's employment agreement."

"That's it," Pie said. "I was wondering why Dubble would take a risk like that just for another job. I could see Hump doing it if he thought he was going to be out on his fanny here, he'da needed something that could pay the alimony..."

"And pay for Mauve," Don put in.

"Yeah. But it didn't make sense for Dubble. He's got a good job at LIT and Bea already explained to me how hard it would be to fire him. He might have made more money at DoTel, but the security wouldn't be there. But stock options in a hot company that's about to go public? That could make him rich."

"He wasn't kidding when he said he was a loser. I'm almost sorry for him. Almost."

"The question is," Alex said, "whether he knew his clock was getting fixed. If he thought Hump was legitimately pushing papers, he doesn't have a motive. Hump's death makes him a loser. If he got wind of what Hump was up to, he's got one helluva motive. Once the papers got into the system, his career was stopped right where it is."

"That's not much of a motive," Don said. "He's making a good living now and he's not too far from retirement."

"Depends on how Dubble looks at things. Do any of us know what's really important to him?"

The three of us looked at one another. Shrugged. "Not a hint," Alex told Pie.

"Lemme go back a minute to the question of whether Dubble knew Stafford was doing him dirt. If Dubble saw the papers, would he recognize that it was a set-up, Bea?

"I'm not sure. All of us here would have figured it out sooner or later, but we're all in the management track. Don's in the Senior Executive Service and Alex and I have been government managers. Lee Roy is classified as a computer specialist, which means he has no management responsibilities and no one reports to him. I don't know what he was in his previous incarnations, but it's possible that he's never dealt with personnel and may not know who has to sign off on those things or what qualifications are attached to the various jobs."

"O.K. Let's move on, then. The last point was the red herring. I think we've already covered that. Anything else?"

Don explained the plan for swiping the disks.

"I thought I told you guys not to do anything risky," Pie complained. "You're sailing pretty close to the wind. You already got Dubble's disks, huh?"

"Yeah," Alex said. "I don't think there's any danger here, Pie. We're taking copies of the disks, so I don't see how Dubble or Ben would know anything was gone."

Reluctantly, Pie told us to continue. The only thing that really convinced him was that Don and Alex had already burgled Lee Roy's office. "But don't do anything like that again. And stay in touch. I don't wanna spend the whole week worrying about you. Oh, Bea."

"Yeh?"

"Bring the chart up to date, willya?"

"Sure."

Pie rang off.

By 3 o'clock, Ben had been dispatched; by 3:30 his disks had been copied and replaced. And then nothing for the next two days while Alex took off for an IEEE meeting in Pittsburgh and Don and I spent sun-ups to sun-downs in meetings, budget justifications, program reviews, committee deliberations, contract negotiations and God-knows-what-else.

It wasn't until the week-end that we managed to get to our own particular microcomputers to search our particular stacks of hay for a needle.

CHAPTER 16

March 17 - 19, 1990

The ringing woke me up and I groped for the alarm clock. I pushed all the buttons I could find with my eyes closed, but the ringing went on. I pondered for a while and came to the conclusion that the sound was emanating either from the door-bell or the telephone. Analysis indicated the telephone. I opened my eyes to a pitch black room. I turned on the light and found the phone. "Bea Goode speaking."

A voice on the other end muttering to someone else. "This is the right one." And to me, "Miss Goode? I'm calling from George Washington Hospital. Miss Frances Monk has had a massive stroke. I'm sorry to bother you at this hour, but she's in critical condition and she's been asking for you."

"Frances? Asking for me? Shall I come right over?"

"If you would, I'm sure it would ease her mind." The voice told me where to find Frances. As I was about to hang up, it asked, "Miss Goode, do you know what Miss Monk's religion is?"

"I'm sorry, no. I don't really know anything about her. I'll be there as soon as I can."

I looked at the clock. 5:15. I got dressed, brushed my teeth, and ran for my car. There was no traffic at that hour of the morning and I bowled along the Boulevard at a fair clip. If they were asking about Frances' religion, they must be pessimistic about her chances of survival. Why had she asked for me? Was she going to confess to knocking off Hump? Why would she want to confess to me? Who else was there?

I abandoned, rather than parked, my car, ran into the hospital, and up to Frances' floor. The floor nurse hurried me to the room. "She's hard to understand," she said, "but she can speak. She's been very agitated; please try to soothe her. Poor lady."

Frances was lying, white-faced, in the hospital bed. The left side of her face was drawn down, eyelid closed, half of her lips drooping. Her left arm was motionless on top of the counterpane. Right hand plucking at the cloth.

I walked around to the right side of the bed and put my hand over hers. "Hello, Dr. Monk."

"Bea?" It came out with a buzz.

"Yes."

"Wan tell somming."

"I'm listening."

"Staffor. Non acciden. Murder. Unstan?"

"Yes. Stafford was murdered. How do you know?"

The right half of Monk's face sketched a smile. "Figger out. By myself. Goo', huh?"

"Very good. How did you figure it out?"

"Smar'. I'm smar'. Robes don do by selves. Unstan?"

"Yes. Robots don't act by themselves. Do you know who made the robot do it?"

"Staffor no goo'. Shou'n kill anyway. Bad to do.""

"Very bad. Do you know who did it?"

"Don know. Nee' more time. Figger out. I'm smar'. Nee' time. No' nuff time." She closed her right eye and said no more.

"I think she'll sleep now, Miss Goode. Thank you so much for coming right over. We'll keep you informed."

I left the hospital and rescued my car. Poor Frances. How much of her life was spent among strangers? I wondered if she'd live long enough to get her award. Hoped so. So she'd figured out that Hump had been murdered. How many other people had come to that conclusion? Probably everyone who thought about it at all. Except the police. Even they might be playing an undercover game. And of those who had come to the murder conclusion -- how many were doing a spot of detecting? Now there's a mind-boggling thought!

The eastern sky was beginning to hint of a sunrise. I pulled up to my house at 6:30. I put on the coffee and pulled some Danishes out of the freezer. Showered, ate, and settled down to my share of disks.

The unlabeled disks were useless as an aid to detection but for purposes of character analysis, they had merit. Ben, methodical as always, had formatted his disks, ready for instant action. In fact, he had a box and a half of formatted disks. Nothing on them, however.

Lee Roy, disgusting as always, had some material on his disks that would have made a sea-parrot blush. On discovering that his disks were not blank, I decided to try to decipher them before calling Alex. On the chance that the disks contained text, rather than programs, I tried the word processing system and there it all was. Lee Roy had been playing with the graphics writer and had drawn his fantasies in minute detail. Come to think of it, his fantasies weren't all that minute. I took the disk out of the micro and pitched it to one side. It could have been worse. He could have put it on the central computer. Chilling thought: maybe he had put it on the central computer.

Aside from that, nothing. At mid-day, I called Alex to tell him about Monk and to report the unsuccessful culmination of my search. Alex was about a quarter of the way through his allotment and so far had acquired only a headache.

"Do you want me to take a crack at some of your disks?"

"No, thanks. Don and I decided to search them all with Un-erase, just in case the bad guy erased the program without re-formatting."

"I've got some formatted disks among the unlabeled pile that I brought home. Maybe I should try Un-erase on them."

"Nothing visible on them?"

"Nothing of interest," I lied blandly.

"Maybe we should try it. Would you mind bringing them over?"

Uh oh. "Why don't you just loan me Un-erase and I'll look?"

"Bea, it will take me longer to show you how to use it than it will to do it myself."

Trapped. And thus it was that on Saturday afternoon I carted a briefcase full of pornography to Alex's. He was bleary-eyed when I got there, but game. I wandered into the kitchen to make some fresh coffee while Alex scanned disks.

"Bea!"

I turned around. Alex was standing at the kitchen door, a quivering tower of indignation. "You weren't going to tell me what was on those disks, were you?"

I steadied myself against the kitchen counter.

"No."

"The only break in a migraine-producing weekend and you weren't going to tell me!"

I couldn't help it. I collapsed, laughing helplessly. It took all of two seconds for Alex to join me.

Eventually, we stopped laughing, drank coffee, and made love. It was a nice, comfortable love. After which we just lay there, enjoying being together.

"Alex?"

" Hmmm?"

"I gave you my life's story. Now tell me who you are."

"Story's not too different from yours, except that my parents didn't die until I was in grad school. Only child. Middle class background. A couple of buddies I still keep in touch with, but we don't have much in common. They did things like go into retail or dentistry or something like that."

I mulled that over. Retail or dentistry or something like that? The similarity escaped me but computer scientists see links where the rest of us see voids. "So what made you be a computer scientist?'

"When I was in high school - second year - they had this science fair and a bunch of scientists came to judge it. There weren't any desk top computers at the time, just great big things that used punch cards. I had cajoled one of my dad's acquaintances, a banker, into helping me make a little program and running it on the bank's machine. I entered it in the fair and one of the judges, a little French guy, got fascinated with it - mostly, I think because the bank let me play with its equipment. He worked in the computer lab at John Hopkins and he got me a summer internship every year through my undergraduate days. And the rest, my dear, is history. "

"That's interesting. Do many of the labs take high school interns?"

"I don't know about 'many', but NIST does, and the Naval Research Lab, and a few places at the National Institutes of Health. George Washington U. has a summer program where they select kids and send them to the labs where they get mentored by a scientist. Then at the end of the summer all of the kids submit their work and the Washington Academy of Sciences hands out prizes. My little French guy organizes the judging and prize giving."

"How come LIT doesn't take some interns?"

"Hump nixed it. Said we were too new and had to mature before we took anything like that on."

"Do you agree?'

"Of course not. That was pure bullshit. He just didn't want to be bothered.

"That figures," I muttered.

We finished off the coffee.

Alex was humming 'Brightly Dawns Our Wedding Day' when I finally prepared to go back home.

"Have you revised the chart yet?"

"No, that's on tomorrow's agenda. Do you want to come help me or stick with your disks?"

"What I want," said Alex, "and what I'm going to do are different things. I forgot one stack of disks at the lab. I've got enough to keep me busy today, but I'll go fetch them in the morning. After that, I'd better knuckle down. If we haven't found something by tomorrow evening, why don't we break and go out to dinner?"

"Good thought. About 6:00?"

That settled, I drove home.

Sunday morning began much like Saturday, but not as early. The phone didn't wake me up until 9:00 -- when I should have been up anyway. News of Monk? "Bea Goode speaking."

"Freddie Langsteth, Bea. Something's come up. Wondered if I could drop by and talk."

Oh, dear.

"Bea? Too early to call?"

"Uh, no, Freddie. I'm expecting some people shortly, though. I'll call and tell them you're coming over. They can come a little later."

"Sure? We can make it another time."

"No, that's o.k." I gave Freddie directions, hung up, and called Alex. No answer. He must have left for his lab. I called Don.

"Freddie Langsteth is on her way over here. Can you come over and provide some protection in case she's of murderous intent?" I didn't feel nearly as flippant as I sounded.

"Bea, are you crazy? She's a suspect. Why'd you invite her over?"

"I didn't, she invited herself. I thought Alex could get here before she did -- she's coming from the District -- but Alex isn't home."

"I'll come, but it'll take me an hour to get there from here. What're you going to do in the meantime?"

"I told Freddie that I was expecting people and that I was going to call and tell them she's coming. Even if she has murder in mind, that should give her pause."

"I'll be there as soon as I can. You're an idiot." Don rang off.

The man was right. I didn't think that Freddie was the bad guy; I couldn't see any way that she could have done it. Or if she had, why she would want to do me in. Nonetheless, Don was right. I was an idiot.

While waiting for Freddie, I located various objects in the house that I could use as makeshift weapons. Then I located various things I could hide behind. I tried Alex again. The dum-dum still wasn't home.

The doorbell finally rang and there was Freddie. She was carrying a cake box. "Not much open today. Thought I'd better bring something since I invited myself." We went into the kitchen and I put on a fresh pot of coffee and opened the box. Streusel. Good. We sat down at the dining room table and I waited for Freddie to take the first bite. She did not fall over dead nor did I.

"Sorry to bother you like this, Bea, but I don't know anyone else in this town to talk to. Worried."

"I know the feeling. What's wrong?"

Freddie stirred her coffee and looked around. I found her an ashtray. "Thanks. Stafford must have been murdered."

I nodded. "Everyone seems to have figured that out." I told her about Monk.

"Sad. World's full of sad stories. It's my sad story that's worrying me, though. Had an affair with Stafford a few years ago. Before he married Her Dumbness. He ditched me. Not to put too fine a point on it." Freddie smiled, wryly. "No hope of keeping it secret in Washington. Damndest town I ever saw. No one knows anyone but they tell everyone everything. Won't ask if you'd heard about our great affair."

And a good thing. I don't know what I would have said.

"Wouldn't have told you now, except that's what's worrying me."

I cut some more streusel. "Why should that worry you after all this time?"

Freddie swallowed some coffee to wash down the cake. "Motive. Story'll get out. People'll think I killed the sonofabitch."

"Did you?" A front-runner for the Dumb-Assed Question of the Year Award.

Freddie gave me a look. "For the record, no. Also for the record, you're an idiot." Unanimity -- isn't it wonderful.

"If you thought I killed the prick why'd you let me in the front door?"

"I don't think you killed him. I just thought I'd ask."

Freddie started to laugh and choked on her streusel. I got up and pounded her on the back for a while.

"I don't see why people should think you killed Hump. You weren't anywhere near the LIT building that day, were you?"

"No. Out of town, in fact. Site visit to one of the DoTI field offices. Do you know how it was done? Did the killer have to be there?"

"I would assume so. Have you figured out a method?"

She shook her head. "No, but I don't know how those things work. Robots are operated remotely, but I don't know how remotely. Mysterious technology."

"I'm not any more knowledgeable than you are. They made me learn how to program in Basic when I was getting my graduate degree, but I haven't used it from that day to this."

"You're one computer language up on me. Resisted all enlightenment. Still think you people ought to do some digging."

"Us? That's what cops do for a living."

"Hmph. Carfil's in deep shit unless someone figures out what happened. You trying to tell me that hasn't occurred to you?"

At which point, Don and Connie arrived.

Hellos, introductions, and good-byes.

Freddie grinned at me on the way out. "Glad to know LIT's working on it. No one else has a Chinaman's chance of figuring it out. No pun intended." We heard her car start up and be gone.

"Honestly, Bea," Connie said, helping herself to some streusel, "don't you have any sense of self preservation? You've narrowed your suspect list down to less than a dozen and you invite one of them over for coffee! You need a keeper."

I was beginning to get sick of that theme. "You're right. Do you want to sleep here until it's over?"

Don laughed. "Connie doesn't, but I think I could get Alex to volunteer." He popped the last of the cake in his mouth.

"Shut up and have some coffee. How's that for grace under pressure?"

Connie thought for a bit. "Needs work. What else is new?"

We spent the next hour talking about Frances Monk and then it was time to go. Connie put her arm on my shoulder. "I'm sorry I lectured you. I was worried."

"I deserved it. It was good of you both to drop everything and rush over." It really was.

I washed up the coffee things and settled down to the chart. Had this past few days changed anything? Not so far as Don and John were concerned. Monk? Not really if all you were looking at was the chart. But a deathbed statement couldn't be taken lightly. Or could it? Either Frances thought she was dying or she thought she would live. If the former, she might not want "Murderer" as an epitaph even if she was one. If she thought she would live, then it wasn't a deathbed statement. No matter which, her line in the chart remained unchanged.

Lee Roy? Still no idea whether he knows Ada. Motive gets murky. Do it logically. Suppose he didn't know what Hump was up to and thought he had been rejected for the DoTel job because Hump was in the way. Motive Number 1, then, remains ambition. I made a note on the chart. Suppose he had given up on the DoTel job but didn't know that Hump was out to "fix his clock". In that case, no motive. Next, suppose he had given up on the Do-Tel job and was perfectly aware of what Hump was up to. Motive Number 2 becomes vengeance. I made the note. Any more? With Hump gone, those career-killing papers wouldn't get into the system. But Lee Roy thought the papers were already in the system. According to Lee Roy. It was a thin motive, in any event, but added to the other two, it could have tipped the scales. From Dubble's peculiar perspective, Hump's death would certainly maximize the chances of something good happening. I finished my notes on Lee Roy.

Stevie. Confirmed that Hump had indeed buried his papers. I couldn't imagine that Steve would knock him off for that. Even assuming that Steve knew that the papers hadn't been moved and was boiling mad about it, he would certainly have pursued some avenue short of homicide. Like having a roaring fight with Hump. On the other hand, who's to say that he hadn't? Maybe we just hadn't known about it. But this wasn't a killing done in a fit of murderous passion. It had been coldly planned and carefully executed. Ambition as a motive for Steve was ridiculous. I wrote it down anyway, then added a question mark.

Who else? Nothing new on Ben or Gus. Freddie? She said she doesn't know any computer languages. I was inclined to believe her. But my inclinations weren't facts. I penciled in an "N" with a question mark. She has a checkable alibi for the opportunity column -- unlikely to offer it if it weren't true.

Finally, Mauve. If my guess was right and she had lured me over to her place to rat out Lee Roy, then she was perfectly capable of giving me a load of codwallop about pining to move to Denver as the Gracious Lady. If that were the case, then Hump's insurance and pension would be adequate motives, thank you. Would Hump's former wife get a share of that? I didn't think so and Mauve sure didn't sound like she thought it would be shared. And she had talked to a lawyer. So far as I could see, that was the best motive in town. Unfortunately, she didn't fit the rest of the profile. I took one more look at the chart and erased "jealousy" in Mauve's motive column. No smell of anything like it.

For all of the activity of the past few days, we hadn't got much forrader, chart-wise.

Name	Ada?	Opportunity		Motive	Lox?
		Bldg.	Roof		
Don	Y	Y	N	Patriotism	N
John	Y	Y	N	Ambition	N
Monk	?	Y	N	Afraid of losing job	N
Lee	Y?	Y	Y	Ambition	Y
Roy					
Steve	Y	Y	Y	Ambition	Y
Ben	Y	Y	Y	Afraid of losing job	Y
Gus	Y	Y	N	Vengeance, hope Case	N

				will be dropped	
Freddie	N?	N	N	Vengeance	?
Mauve	N	N	N	Inheritance?	Y
				Jealousy?	

Pie called about 4:00 to tell me that Aunt Bessie was flying up from the Yucatan. She would land in Boston at 8:00. I gave him the news of the day and collapsed in front of the tv set. Crawling out of a hole three-years deep was exhausting. Was it only a month ago that I was complaining about feeling lonely?

At 5:30 I took a long, warm shower, doused myself with cologne, dressed, and settled down to wait for Alex. At 6:15 the usually punctual Alex had not arrived. I wondered if he had found something on one of the disks and become engrossed. At 6:20, I called him. No answer; he must be on his way. Still no Alex at 6:30. At 6:40 I caught the telephone on its first ring.

It was Pie. "Sit down, Bea."

I froze. "Pie, what is it?"

"Alex is in the hospital. He was shot in front of his house."

My mouth was dry.

"Bea?"

"I'm here," I managed to get the words out. "Is he alright? Pie, he's not going to..." I couldn't get *that* word out.

"Bea, listen. He's at Alexandria General. I don't know how bad it is. I'm going to meet Bessie at the airport and we'll take the next plane out to Washington. You go to the hospital and we'll meet you there as soon as we can." Pie hung up.

I got my coat and stumbled out to the car. I turned on the motor and sat there, dully, until I realized that I hadn't any idea where Alexandria General was. I went back into the house and looked it up in the phone book. Somehow, I got to the hospital and, eventually, to the floor where Alex's room was. The floor nurse was sitting behind a small desk. "I'm Beatrice Goode. Alex Carfil's fiancee."

She smiled at me, sympathetically. "He's still in intensive care, Miss Goode. Why don't you sit down in the waiting room. We'll let you know as soon as they bring him up."

I forced myself to ask. "Will he be alright?"

The nurse looked at her notes. "I'll ask the doctor to come see you as soon as he's available."

Oh, God. Alex, don't die. I went to the waiting room and sat down. After a while, Don and Connie arrived. Pie had called them. We didn't talk. I couldn't. I just sat there, blindly. At last the doctor came.

Alex had been shot, presumably by someone with robbery in mind. His attacker, wearing a ski mask, was bending over Alex's bleeding body when a neighbor came out to walk his dog. The dog barked; the attacker fled; the dog, who apparently was something of a pussycat, hid behind his master until they both went back into the house and the man dialed 911.

The bullet had hit Alex in the midsection. Fortunately, it was a little bullet -- a .22 -- and had missed the vital organs but Alex had lost a great deal of blood. His condition was critical.

My mind kept replaying the despair of three years ago. I was in a hospital bed and Harry was dead. Over and over. Finally, I went numb.

It was almost 11:00 when Pie and Bessie arrived. Bessie sat beside me on the couch and put her arms around me. The numbness wore off and I cried. "Aunt Bessie, I can't do this again. I can't." Bessie held me tighter.

At midnight, a nurse arrived. Alex was still in some peril, but things looked brighter. They were bringing him upstairs. No visitors, not until tomorrow.

I really looked at Bessie for the first time since she had arrived. She was the same little apple dumpling that I had abandoned three years ago -- a bit browner. We hugged and kissed and I tried to introduce her to Don and Connie -- an act of courtesy that Pie had performed an hour ago.

"Excuse me," the nurse said, "but the patient will probably need his toiletries and perhaps some pajamas. The men don't like these hospital gowns."

"If you've got his keys, I can run over to his house and get them," I volunteered.

"I'll see if his keys are among his things. Why don't you all go home tonight? He won't wake up until morning." She went off to find the keys.

"Look," I said, "why don't you take her advice? I'll get Alex's things and come back here. If there's any change, I'll phone you." I took my house key from its ring and handed it to Bessie. "You've been traveling all day, you must be exhausted. You and Pie can stay at my place."

"Bea," she said, "I can always sleep. Pie and I will go with you." She tried unsuccessfully to stifle a yawn.

"I'm alright, Aunt Bessie, really. As long as you guys are on the end of the phone."

"She's right, Bess." Pie took Bessie's arm. "You'll call us as soon as you hear something, Bea?"

"Of course. You, too." To Don and Connie. They all kissed me and they left. The nurse came back with Alex's key ring. "This one looks like a house key," she said, holding it out.

"I'd better take the whole ring, just in case."

I took the keys, found my car, and drove to Alex's.

I had a bad moment when I approached the stain where Alex had lain, bleeding. I stepped around it and put the key in the lock. The nurse was right. It fit.

I found Alex's toothbrush and razor and then rummaged around in the bedroom, collecting two pairs of pajamas, slippers, and the scruffy bathrobe. I'd have to get him a new one.

Then I went into the study, where Alex's microcomputer held place of honor. I sat down and cried some more. Come on, Bea, he's a healthy animal. Nothing essential was hit. If he's survived the loss of blood so far he'll be o.k. I think.

I looked around for some books and scooped up an armful of paperbacks. P.D. James. MRF Keating. Colin Dexter. Ellis Peters. Reginald Hill. Sarah Caudwell. Tony Hillerman. All classic whodunits. Not a single kick-em-in-the-guts among them. My lovely gentle Alex. I'll get him some more cozies tomorrow. Meanwhile, he can re-read these. I hope.

Next to the computer was a neat stack of the disks that Alex had been examining. Next to the stack was a single disk, unlabeled and alone. I picked it up. Had Alex found something?

Robbery my Aunt Fanny. We should have listened to Pie. Who knew Alex had the disks?

I drove back to the hospital with Alex's things and settled down on the waiting room couch. Someone shook me. A nurse -- a different one.

"Miss Goode? Mr. Carfil is awake if you want to see him for a minute."

Did I! I followed the nurse into Alex's room. Alex was ashen. He had tubes stuck virtually every place there was to stick a tube. He looked absolutely marvelous; he was breathing. I went over to the bed and kissed him gingerly. Alex smiled faintly, "Watch it, klutz," he whispered, "I need these tubes." He closed his eyes and went back to sleep.

The nurse motioned to me. "He's really not supposed to have visitors yet. It's just that you've been waiting so long..." Her voice trailed off.

"You want me to get out?"

She nodded. "He really won't be fully conscious until later this afternoon. Why don't you go home and wash up and come back about 3:00."

I called home from the hospital. Pie answered and I gave him the promising news.

"Whoosh," he said. "*Mazeltov*. When can he have visitors?"

"The nurse threw me out and told me to come back at 3:00. Alex was pretty much out of it when I saw him. But alive, Pie, alive!"

"Did you talk with the police? Are they sure this was just a random attack and isn't connected to the robot business?"

"I haven't talked with them, but I think they're sure. It doesn't have the feel of Hump's murder. I mean, a guy who's gone through that really meticulous planning is unlikely to pop off someone with a .22."

"You may be right, but don't discount it altogether. By the way, I called the other hospital about Monk. Thought I'd go see her, but they're not allowing visitors. Bad business."

There was some muffled conversation on the other end of the line. "Listen, Bea, will you be o.k. for a couple of days if we go back to Boston? We'll both come back on Wednesday."

"Sure." Oddly enough, that was true.

"O.K., if we leave now, we might be able to catch the 7:00 flight. Are you going into the office?"

"I hadn't thought about it. I suppose so. I want to get cleaned up first, though."

"Would you mind calling your friends on the Hill and finding out if I should go see someone before the confirmation hearings? I'd better start doing something to keep LIT solvent. I'd like Alex to have a place to come back to."

"Be glad to. You'd better get moving if you want to catch that flight. Leave my key in the mailbox."

"O.K. Your Aunt Bessie wants to talk to you."

"Put her on."

"No," said Pie, "we'll miss our plane." He hung up.

I stood looking at the silent receiver until a woman's voice sounded. "If you'd like to make a call, please hang up and...."

So I hung up.

PART III

THE DEBUG ROUTINE

a program that uncovers the errors

CHAPTER 17

March 19 (cont.), 21

I called Don's house as soon as I got home. Connie answered. Don was in the shower. I gave Connie the tidings.

"Bea, that's marvelous. I don't think I've ever worried so much about someone I've never met."

I laughed. "He was worth it, Connie. You'll see when you meet him." I walked upstairs, thought briefly about a shower, and decided that today was my day for sybaritics. I ran a warm bath, added half a bottle of bath oil, and settled in. Eventually the water turned cold and woke me up.

It was 9:30. I plunged into some clothes and ran for the car.

A bright red notebook was sitting in the middle of my desk. I picked it up. At a guess, it weighed 532 pounds and probably contained the minutes of every General Assembly meeting since the inception of the U.N. I opened it to the title page. It was Ben's report. Ginny Jean had finished it. She had put it in a binder. It was over! What on earth would Ben do with his time now? A few occupations crossed my mind and I shuddered. I picked up the binder and lugged it down the hall toward Ben's office. As I passed Stevie's office, I heard him on the phone. "So what if the company's going broke? It's a great computer and someone told me that Xerox is going to pick up the maintenance contracts. You know, like they did with the old Osborne ten years ago. Hey look, I got fifteen of 'em and I'm practically givin' 'em away."

I got to Ben's office and dumped the book on his desk. Slowly, Ben opened the cover to the title page. Ginny Jean had decorated it with little graphic furbelows. Ben paged through the book, stopping once in a while to read a felicitous phrase. A beatific smile spread across his face. "She misspelled 'optimization' every chance she got."

I walked around the desk and looked over Ben's shoulder. There it was. Optimazation. Big as life.

Ben got up. "I'll just take this down to her and..."

"No you won't! Give me the book, Ben, and I'll take care of it." I brought the binder down to the typists' lair and waited for Ginny Jean to finish the sentence she was typing. "Uh, Ginny Jean, the book looks beautiful. You should be proud of it."

"Thank you, Bea," said Ginny Jean.

"Just one thing, though. It shouldn't be too hard to correct if you use the Speller."

"What's that, Bea?" Ginny Jean asked, and fell over, laughing. The rest of the typists joined the merriment. "Hoo hoo hoo," said Ginny Jean, "did Ben, hahaha, see it?"

"See what, Ginny Jean?"

"Optimihoohoohahoo."

"Yes, he saw it."

"Heeheeheeheehee. What did he hoohah say?"

"He pulled his hair and pounded his heels on the floor."

"Hoophoophoop." Ginny Jean slapped the desk. Finally, she recovered and handed me a sheaf of pages. "Here are the pages spelled right. Ben can put them in. Hahahoohoohoop"

I took the pages, carted them and the notebook back to Ben's office and plopped them and the notebook on his desk. "You've made a little girl very happy today," I told him and went back to my office.

Stevie was still trying to peddle the remains of some bankrupt computer company as I walked by.

There was a sheaf of telephone messages on my desk awaiting me. One was from Hope Lahti. Return her call at 225-0001. A Senate exchange. Had Hope found my Senate connection? I dialled.

"Trade and Industry," the voice answered.

"This is Beatrice Goode. I have a message to return Hope Lahti's call at this number."

"One moment please."

"Hope Lahti speaking."

"Hope? This is Bea Goode. What are you doing over in the high rent district?"

Hope tittered. "Guess who's the new staff director?"

"Lahti, you bum! Why didn't you tell me?"

The titter turned into a full-fledged laugh. "I couldn't until the announcement was made. Have you guys figured out what went wrong with the robot?"

"I shouldn't tell you until the announcement is made, but yes. I can't give you any details, but you can tell your Senators that robots are safe for Democracy. We still have some i's to dot before we can release the story."

"Well, you'd better start dotting. Lee's confirmation hearings are coming up in two weeks. Is he as good as his resume?"

"I'm going to have to plead bias on that. He's an old, dear friend of Harry's and mine."

There was a second or two of silence. Then, "Bea, is he the beloved Uncle Pie?"

"You got it in one, Hope."

"Thank heavens it's someone I can work with. Do you think you can persuade him to come down to meet the Chairman before the hearings? He won't have any problems with confirmation in any event, but it sure would help with the budget. I'll have a hard time increasing the mark without him I'm still too new to have the Members' full confidence."

"Do you have a date when he and the Chairman can meet?"

"No. But I can get one this afternoon and call you back."

"O.K. If I'm not here, leave the date and time with the secretary. Pie will be there."

Hope hung up and I let out a triumphant whoop. This had all the earmarks of a great day.

I poked around in my briefcase, extracted the disk that I had taken from Alex's study, and went down the hall to Don's office. He wasn't in. I went back to the reception room where Lenore was pecking away at the word processor. "Where's Don?"

Lenore looked up, smiling pleasantly. "He's at an all-day meeting of the Export Committee. If he calls in, should I tell him you want to speak with him?"

"No. Well, yes. I'm going to leave a little early, though. I'll check out with you."

Lenore nodded and went back to her pecking. I turned to leave.

"Oh, Bea, I forgot. The Memorial Service is next Friday."

"Oh, dear," I said. "When did she die?"

"She?" Lenore looked blank.

"Frances. Dr. Monk."

"Oh, really, Bea. Why would anyone care about a Memorial Service for her? I'm talking about Mr. Stafford." She started to say something else, thought better of it, and closed her mouth.

"Oh. Oh. Yes, of course. I'll tell my staff. Would you send out an all-points notice?"

"Certainly."

I returned to my office. Judging from the absence of hall gossipers, not too many people knew about either Alex or Monk.

I looked at the disk, still clutched in my hand. Should I wait for Don to see what was on it? Should I ask Alex this afternoon? Would Alex be in any condition to answer?

I dialed the hospital. Alex's condition was now listed as 'good'. Visitors later this afternoon. Maybe.

I put the disk in my micro and called up the Directory. 'Tarzan' waved at me. Damn! There was no way for me to tell whether it was the real Tarzan or the kamikaze impostor. Oh yes there was. Alex's key ring was still in my briefcase. I took it out. The little key to the padlocked roof was on it.

I made a copy of the disk, took it out of the micro, and headed for the stairs. I unlocked the padlock and pulled back the bolt. There was no way to replace the padlock from the inside. Just as well. All I needed was for someone to walk by, see it there, and in a fit of Good Citizenship relock it. I could be stuck up on that roof for hours. I took the padlock with me, climbed the stairs, and pushed open the door to the roof. The scene was still set. The monstrous arms were lying center stage, where Alex had left them. The little jar, awaiting its cue, was sitting on the table, the stool beyond it. The mockup was at the perimeter and Alex's micro, on its computer table, was stage left. The huge circus tent that had been thrown up over the whole tableau was echoing the taps of a soft rain. When had the rain started?

I put the padlock on the computer table's recessed shelf, next to Alex's notebook, banged my head on the way up, turned the machine on, put the disk in the drive, and called up Tarzan.

And that's exactly what it was. Plain, old, vanilla Tarzan.

I let the program run for a bit. The arms unscrewed the cap and continued on to its Alex-made route toward the stool. Damn! Alex must have had it off by itself so he wouldn't get it mixed up with the disks we had filched from Lee Roy and Ben. So much for Bea Goode, girl detective.

I turned off the machine, removed the disk from the drive, and picked up the padlock. Decided to look in Alex's notebook to see if there was anything in it he might want to look at while he was hors de combat. Banged my head again. I flipped open the cover and a small, prickly sensation crawled up my spine. It wasn't Alex's notebook and a disk was nestled under the front page. I stared at the disk. Oh, no. Oh, no. Dear God, not him. Make it be just another false alarm.

I sat there staring at the disk. And finally I turned the machine back on, put the disk in the drive, and took a look at the directory. 'Tarzan2' was the only entry. But why would he do it? I typed 'Tarzan2' and the robot arms began to move toward the table. How would he ever live with himself? He was a decent man. One arm picked up the glass jar; the other untwisted the cap. I watched the arms, willing them to go to the stool. They set the jar down, turned toward the stool. I realized that I was holding my breath and let it out in a painful stream. The arms changed direction, and the small arm unflexed. Dear God, why?

I heard footsteps clanging on the metal steps; seven seconds later, a slight noise at the roof door. I looked up. "I don't understand, Steve. Why?"

Stevie was standing there, tears rolling down his cheeks, and pointing a little gun at me. The same gun he used to shoot Alex?

"Aw, Bea, why'd you have to find it? I don't wanna kill you."

"Steve, why did you want to hurt anyone?"

"I had to shoot Alex. Bea, I've been going nuts. That disk was up here and he had the only key to the place. I couldn't get up when the guards were here and then Wilf wouldn't take me up in the elevator. It's a Bittybite disk. Everyone woulda known that I killed Hump. I saw that door unpadlocked and I thought I could sneak up and get it. Jesus, what a mess. And now I gotta kill you."

All the time that Steve was talking I was marveling at how upset he was and how calm I was. Of all the stupid things to think about. Wonderful what shock will do to a person.

"I wasn't asking about Alex, Steve. I figured that out all by myself as soon as I saw the orange disk. Why did you kill Hump?"

"Bea, the guy was selling out his country. There's no reason in the whole goddam world why ZapaCall shouldn't export their stuff. Hump had a deal going with DoTel. He was nothing more than a goddam traitor and he got what he deserved."

Was this Steve Chandler talking? Stevie of the Million Deals? That's when the penny dropped.

"You have money in ZapaCall, haven't you?"

"Yeah, but I wouldn't have killed him just for that. He was selling us out."

"You've been talking with the techies and getting a line on the products that would be recommended for Federal marketing help."

"Yeah. Nothing wrong with that. Anyone can talk to the techies. I told you, that's not why I killed him. You don't think I'd kill someone for money, do you?"

I remembered one of his conversations with his broker. "Your margin was getting called, wasn't it Steve?"

"Bea, cut it out! Stop saying those things."

"You had money with Gus, didn't you?

"Yeah. Lots of it. In pooled investor accounts and once Hump wiped the disk there were no records showing what clients had what investments. And with Gus going to jail I can't get at my money to cover the margin."

The tears were rolling faster. Dear God, why doesn't he pull the trigger and put us both out of our misery. "But Bea, listen. I killed him because he was a traitor. That's why I killed him. Bea, please listen!"

I listened and I heard it -- a plane, rising from National Airport just across the Potomac and turning to follow its route over the LIT building. That's why he hasn't pulled the trigger yet. He's waiting for the noise to cover the sound of the shot, just in case someone might hear. The rain continued to fall on the canvas. Evocative of a sitting duck.

The roar of the plane came nearer, drowning out the sound of the raindrops. It also drowned out the sound of Ben's footsteps as he walked up behind Steve and fetched him a tremendous clout with the big red binder.

I once saw an old film of the second Joe Louis-Max Schmeling fight. Steve went down, classically, just like Schmeling. Ben bent over and picked up the gun. He stood looking at Steve and for a wild minute I thought Ben was going to put one foot on Steve's chest and emit an appropriate

Tarzan victory whoop. I was disappointed. All Ben did was examine the gun and remark, "I wonder what deal he got this thing in?"

"Ben," I said, "did you just deck Steve with your volume of trade statistics?"

"Yes," said Ben, "it figures, doesn't it."

I tried to laugh and realized that I couldn't. I was shaking too hard. Eventually, I managed to control the shakes and left Ben to guard Steve while I called the police. They responded within minutes.. They were considerate and thorough and, best of all, they got Steve out of the building without my having to face him again.

It was nearly 3:00 when the police finished with me and I went off to find Ben. He was sitting on Ginny Jean's desk, being lionized. I walked over and kissed him.

"Thank you, Ben."

His sappy grin broadened.

"Ben, what made you come up to the roof?"

"Oh, I saw the padlock off and went up to see what was going on. I guess that was the key to the whole thing."

I would have forgiven that mutt anything. Even that.

Wednesday evening Pie, Bessie, Don, Connie, and I were clustered around Alex's bedside. He was sitting up, his color much better -- able to hum a few faint bars of 'I'm Called Little Buttercup'. His major problem seemed to be that whenever he thought of Ben braining Steve with the trade statistics, he laughed. And when he laughed, his midsection hurt.

"The next time you do something like this", Bessie remarked, "pick a time when I'm not on a dig. I seem to have missed most of the humor. Anyway, when are you going to get married?" Bessie's digging was not confined to archeological expeditions.

Alex looked at me. "As soon as I get out of here, unless Bea has some objection."

"She doesn't have an objection. So. You'll all come up to Boston and get married in our house? It would be nice to have a wedding there before we rent the place and move to Washington."

"Aunt Bessie, Pie can't give me away again. I'd feel like an unwanted kitten that crawled back home."

Pie crossed his elegantly clad legs. "So, *nu*? By this time you're a cat. Listen to your aunt, Bea."

"Don," Alex asked, "will you be best man?"

"I'd be honored." Don looked as if he meant it. "Just don't schedule the wedding on a softball practice night."

"Don!" Connie looked scandalized. "You know," she said, "what I still don't understand is why Steve left that disk up on the roof in the first place. Why didn't he just take it with him?"

"That was bothering me, too," Pie said. "It's not something he would have forgotten."

"Naw," Don said. "What happened was that he sent Ben down to lunch and to ask Delamain to bring up his jacket and briefcase. I'll bet Delamain would've had to look around for the briefcase. That would give Chandler time to erase the disk and put it in his notebook."

"Right," Alex cut in. "Then when John brought the stuff up Steve would have casually retrieved his notebook from the computer table, slipped it into his jacket pocket or briefcase and left for lunch with it. I wondered why he went up to the roof without his jacket. It was blustery up there. He probably wanted to make sure that whoever brought the stuff up didn't decide he could get his own briefcase. It was less likely that they'd let him freeze." He shook his head. "It never occurred to me to look on the little shelf when I was up there trying to figure out what happened."

Don continued, "Lee Roy screwed up the plan by coming up while John was getting the stuff. Steve must have heard him clumping up the metal stairs, pulled the disk, and scooted to the mock-up side of the roof so that whoever was coming up would see him innocently arranging the set. Without the jacket or briefcase he wouldn't have had a handy pocket to put the disk in, so he slipped it into the notebook and pitched it onto the shelf. I don't think you could get a match in those trouser pockets of his. He probably hoped he could get back to the computer table afterwards. Between Lenore's hysterics and the quick reaction of the security guards, that hope was squashed."

"Well," said Pie. "At last I know what Dubble's good for. Don't tell him. He'll want me to give him an award."

Alex started to laugh and grabbed his belly. I put my arms around him.

"So stop, already," said Bessie. "You'll give him a relapse. Who do you want at the wedding?"

"Ben," Alex and I said.

"That's all?" asked Bessie. "That's some wedding."

A tactful 'ahem' sounded from the doorway.

And there was Ben, in pink and brown polyester tweed, bearing a hideous, huge gloxinia plant. He considered the tableau before him and shrugged.

"Well," he said, "if you can't Bea Goode, Bea Carfil."

Made in the USA
Charleston, SC
30 July 2012